CROSSING VALUES

CROSSING VALUES

by
Carrie Daws

Ambassador International
GREENVILLE, SOUTH CAROLINA & BELFAST, NORTHERN IRELAND
www.ambassador-international.com

CROSSING VALUES

Printed in the United States of America

ISBN: 9781935507925
eISBN: 9781935507956

Cover Design by Matthew Mulder
Page Layout by Kelley Moore of Points & Picas

AMBASSADOR INTERNATIONAL
Emerald House
427 Wade Hampton Blvd.
Greenville, SC 29609, USA
www.ambassador-international.com

AMBASSADOR BOOKS
The Mount
2 Woodstock Link
Belfast, BT6 8DD, Northern Ireland, UK
www.ambassador-international.com

The colophon is a trademark of Ambassador

And I pray that you, being rooted and established in love, may have power, together with all the Lord's holy people, to grasp how wide and long and high and deep is the love of Christ, and to know this love that surpasses knowledge—that you may be filled to the measure of all the fullness of God. Now to him who is able to do immeasurably more than all we ask or imagine, according to his power that is at work within us, to him be glory in the church and in Christ Jesus throughout all generations, for ever and ever! Amen.

Ephesians 3:17b–21

Chapter I

CHARMING TOWN, Amber Griffin thought as she kicked a plod of snow and walked past a sign welcoming her to Crossing, Oregon, population 725. Many homes featured broad porches, picket fences, and snowmen of various sizes. As she considered snatching a carrot nose for breakfast, she thought, *This is the kind of town where everyone knows everyone and you expect Sheriff Taylor to stroll down Main Street.*

Stepping over an abandoned mitten, she paused to watch two girls playing with dolls on the other side of a picture window. Her eyes lingered on the hearth and the fire burning in it. "If only people were as reliable in person as they are on TV," she muttered.

As homes gave way to storefronts, Amber came upon a park that seemed to be the town's center. She walked to the nearest bench, brushed snow off the seat, and eased her frigid muscles onto it. She stomped her feet, her toes aching in response. *At least I know they're not frostbitten.*

With no good options the night before, Amber had forced her way into a dilapidated cabin a few miles outside of town. The thin mattress and worn quilt she'd found made sleep difficult in the plummeting temperatures, but the walls had kept the snow off of her. She'd slept in worse places.

An old Ford F150 rumbled down the street, blowing its horn at two boys practicing wrap-arounds with their hockey sticks. The boys waved in response just before the truck stopped at the hardware store. As a gray-haired man got out of the truck, Amber noticed a small yellow cross on the tailgate.

Next to the hardware store was a Christmas tree lot with a large sign promising to have trees ready by November 28th. *Is that next Friday or Saturday?* Amber wondered, trying to think back to when she last knew the date.

Across the street she could see a barber shop, a diner advertising lunch specials, and a two-story lawyer's office with a couple of jeeps parked in front. A woman stepped out of the law office and Amber watched her follow the sidewalk around the square to enter the General Store. *Now what kind of legal troubles could that Barbie doll have?*

An ice cream shop and the local newspaper sat quietly next to the General Store. *Quite a variety in this little area. Maybe someone will let me stock shelves.*

Amber forced herself to get up off the bench and cross the street to Micah's Hardware. Rock salt crunched under her shoes as she mounted the steps of the blue storefront. She stepped inside, taking a moment to stomp her feet on the rough welcome mat. As warm air enveloped her, she noticed walls covered in tools. Aisles lined the middle of the old wood floor, all angled to guide people to the front counter. She suddenly realized how quiet the store was and looked to see two men leaning on the counter, staring at her.

"Can I help you?" The man behind the counter straightened as he spoke. His blue jean overalls hung limply around his thin frame, and his light blue shirt echoed the icy color of his eyes.

Amber swallowed hard, balling her fists to help her summon the remnant of courage left in her. "I'm wondering if you need any help around the store."

"It's a bit slow this time of year. Can't say I really need much help." His eyes narrowed slightly.

Amber nibbled on her bottom lip. Her skin was beginning to prickle in the warm air and her muscles relax. She pushed herself to ask, "Do you know of anyone in town that may be hiring? Just for a few weeks," she quickly added. "I'm not looking for anything permanent."

"If you mean to stay out the winter, I could use some help."

Amber tore her eyes from the tight line of the first man's face to look at the second man. A good seven or eight inches taller than her slight five-foot, two-inch frame, he had the look of working outdoors, with his jeans, work boots, and weathered face, despite a roundness to his midsection. About the same age as the first man, he resembled an older John Walton from the popular television show. *Almost trustworthy,* she thought.

"I could probably hang around for three or four months, depending on the job."

"My wife and I own a small loggin' business just outside of town," the man continued. "I'd like her to have some company 'round the office while the rest of us are busy elsewhere. Truth be told, she ain't the best at keepin' up with the paperwork, and you'd be takin' a load off my shoulders if you could help with that."

"How far is that from here?" *An office job would certainly be better than that last dishwashing job!*

"Oh, 'bout ten miles," he said. "Job includes room and board if that's what you're wonderin'. You can stay in our extra room and eat all your meals with us. Your evenin's and weekends would be yours to do with what you want."

Amber hesitated. This sounded too good to be true, and in her experience that only brought trouble.

"You could always try it out for a few days. If it ain't to your likin', then I'll bring you right back here."

Amber shifted her weight from one foot to the other. *It's only for a few weeks, and I can leave if it's not what he says.* "Okay. I'll give it a try."

"Good. Name's Frank Yager and my truck's parked right out front."

<hr />

Frank turned his old Ford into a snow-covered driveway and Amber stared in disbelief. The worn-out truck with the faded paint and squeaky bench seat they were riding on hadn't prepared her for this two-story log cabin.

It looks like a magazine cover! "That's your house?"

"Yeah. Didn't seem like so much when all the kids were little. Seems too big now. Too quiet, I s'pose."

Red Ace Potentilla bushes covered the landscaping around the deck that extended the full length of the house. Smoke curled out of the chimney near the back of the house, casting a slight haze on darkening skies. Noble firs towered over the home's back corners, and an Oregon maple stood bare of leaves in the front yard.

Frank drove into the middle bay of a three-car garage. Amber stepped out of the truck, chilly air hitting her as she noticed a lavish Grand Cherokee beside her and a black Camry behind

Frank. She glanced out the open garage door and looked warily at the snow.

A warm bed is worth giving this man and his job a try, she reminded herself.

Frank motioned Amber forward and reached to take her faded backpack from her. "How 'bout we get you settled in? I'll get you introduced to my wife, Faye, and Peter if he's inside. He's our younger son."

Amber nodded, beginning to move forward, and then halted just past the front of the truck. A medium-sized Australian Shepherd barred her pathway. It growled then barked a warning. Amber didn't move. *Not again!*

"Sassy! Get on with ya now!" Frank came up to Amber's side. Amber remained frozen in place.

A door opened behind the dog. "Dad?"

"Peter, get Sassy for us, will ya?"

Peter bent down to grab the dog's collar, talking gently into its dark brown ear. The dog remained watchful but obediently sat upon Peter's command.

"Sorry 'bout that, Amber. Let's get you properly introduced and then Sassy'll let you be. She loves people but is a bit careful 'round strangers."

Amber barely nodded, her eyes fixed on the dog. *Running doesn't do any good. She'll catch me.*

"This is our son, Peter Yager." Frank motioned to her, her backpack dangling from his hand. "Amber's gonna be stayin' with us for a bit, helpin' your mom out at the office."

Peter commanded the dog to stay then stood to offer his hand to Amber. "It's nice to meet you." Amber gingerly took his hand for a quick shake. Just an inch or two taller than his father,

Peter looked to be in his late twenties. His jeans and tan sweater with a white T-shirt peeking out of the top didn't show any hint of a potbelly like Frank's. But still they were clearly related, sharing the same straight nose, angular jaw, and easy grin.

"As soon as Sassy knows you're welcome here, she'll leave you alone," said Peter.

Again Amber nodded, darting a look at him then refocusing on the dog.

Frank led the way up two steps into a mudroom. Amber watched Sassy bound past him and jump through a dog door into the house before she followed Frank. Peter closed the garage behind them before asking, "May I take your coat, Amber?"

She eyed him carefully before silently removing her coat and handing it to him. He hung it on a post next to several down-filled winter coats and wool-lined hats. Frank sat down on one of two long benches lining the room and began to untie his shoes.

"Faye likes for us to take our outside shoes off before we go inside. I try to 'bide her wishes. She's got more time to make those pies of hers if she don't have so much cleanin' up to do!" Frank winked a sparkling eye at her and Peter grinned.

"It's not like Momma doesn't look for excuses to bake as it is, Dad."

"True 'nough. But there's no sense in makin' a mess that'll keep her out of the kitchen."

Amber sat down to remove her worn boots while the two men patiently waited for her. *Good thing the truck warmed up my fingers*, she thought as she fumbled with the laces.

"Peter! Was that your dad?" A door to Amber's left popped open and an older woman appeared. "Oh, goodness! Who do we have here?"

"Love, this here's Amber. Amber, my wife, Faye."

"So that's what Sassy was excited about!" said Faye. "It's so nice to meet you."

Amber stood, trying to avoid the wet spots on the rubber floor. Faye reminded her of a sweet grandmother, slightly plump and full of joy. As she smiled broadly, each part of her face seemed to participate, from her dancing eyes to her dimpled cheeks. *Does she seriously react like this to every stranger?*

"You must stay for dinner. I have a big pot of beef stew that's been simmerin' all afternoon. It's simply too much for the three of us and I won't have so much left over that we're forced to eat it all the way to Thanksgiving." Faye reached for Amber's hand and Amber reminded herself not to stiffen as Faye gently led her into the house.

"Now what brings you to Crossin', Amber?" said Faye. "We don't see many new people stopping through this part of Oregon, you know."

Faye walked Amber through a kitchen smelling of fresh bread. As they passed a set of circular stairs, Faye guided Amber around an overstuffed leather couch facing a wall of windows. The two women sat down, the spectacular view of the Cascade Mountains dimming in comparison to the blaze in the fireplace to Amber's right.

Wouldn't it be nice to sit by that fire! thought Amber.

"I ran into Amber at Micah's lookin' for work." Frank sat down in a matching leather chair to Amber's right, closest to the fire. "I was thinkin' she could help out at the office, maybe keep you some company here when Pete and I are down at the mill or in the shop."

"Oh, wonderful! Have you worked in an office before, dear?" Faye looked at Amber expectantly, pushing up the sleeves on her sweatshirt.

"No." Amber nibbled on her bottom lip.

"Well, that's all right. Sometimes the best way to learn is to dive in with both feet. I bet you pick up on most of it quickly. None of it's really that complicated."

Amber nodded, then looked down at her hands.

"Do you know anything about logging, Amber?"

She jumped at Peter's voice. He'd sat down on the arm of the chair to her left.

"No," she said as she shifted uncomfortably on the lush couch. She eyed the dog sitting quietly on the floor at Peter's feet.

"Don't worry your pretty head about that," said Faye. "I didn't either when Frank brought us out here. Born and raised in the city, I was, and didn't know a thing about living in the middle of nowhere."

"I told Amber she could stay upstairs and eat with us too. I figure there's no sense in her tryin' to find a place in town when we got plenty here."

"Oh, Amber! Of course you must stay here." Faye gently squeezed her hand as Amber forced a smile. "We have a room that's hardly used, and quite honestly some female company would be nice. You can help me keep the men 'round here in order."

Frank snorted. "I'll grant you'll like the female company plenty. But you, love, need little help in keepin' the men 'round here in order." Frank grinned broadly. "Don't let her fool you one bit, Amber. Most the men 'round here would walk to town in a blizzard if Faye asked it of 'em."

Amber heard Peter chuckle but he kept quiet.

"Oh, really, Frank. A blizzard?"

Amber looked from Faye to Frank and back again. She noticed Faye's eyes sparkling in response to Frank's grin. *The banter sounds playful, but . . .*

"Very near to it, love. And you know it."

Faye turned to face Amber again. "Don't you believe but about every other word he says. Tell you what. Peter, take Amber upstairs and show her where the guest room is. And please make sure there's plenty of towels in that bathroom. Frank, you go get yourself cleaned up while I finish the biscuits and we'll all meet at the table for dinner. Okay?"

Chapter 2

PETER LED AMBER UP THE circular staircase, Sassy keeping beside him. At the top, he turned to the right and opened a door into a spacious bedroom with its own sitting area overlooking the same mountains that could be seen from the couch downstairs. Peter hadn't entered the room since they'd moved his sister Brittney to Portland. He'd forgotten how the springtime look with purple and white pansies contrasted against the harsh winter scene outside the windows.

Peter set Amber's backpack down on the bed and turned to look at her. She seemed a bit shell-shocked. Her red flannel shirt accented gold flecks in her brown eyes, but her long brown hair fell lifeless from her side part, showing no trace of the bounce he was used to seeing in Brittney's auburn hair.

"This was my sister's room. Hopefully all the purple doesn't bother you. It's always been her favorite color."

"It's fine."

Not much more than a whisper, thought Peter. He pointed out the door back toward the stairs they'd just climbed. "The bathroom is that open door right at the top of the stairs. Towels and all are on the shelves by the tub. I normally run before breakfast and shower after, so it's all yours before 8:00 a.m."

"Okay."

"If you need anything, just ask. Mom normally keeps all kinds of things on hand for visitors."

"Thanks."

Another one-word sentence. She certainly doesn't make conversation easy. "Well, I'll let you get settled." He took a couple steps toward the door. "Brittney may have left a few clothes in one of the drawers or the closet. She likes to keep some things here in case she needs them when she comes down. Feel free to push them aside. She won't mind."

Amber just nodded at him and mumbled something that sounded like "thank you." Standing motionless just inside the door by the dresser, she wouldn't quite look at him but was keeping a close watch on Sassy's movements. Peter called Sassy to him and directed her out the door.

"Do dogs bother you, Amber?"

"Huh?"

"Sass, go find Momma." Peter watched Sassy look back at Amber then obediently head out the door. He turned in time to see Amber relax slightly. "If dogs bother you, we can keep Sassy away. She tends to follow me, but she can stay downstairs with Mom and Dad if that would make you more comfortable."

"It's okay."

Amber's face was very expressive, but he'd only seen discomfort, fear, and uncertainty. "Let me know if you change your mind. It's not a problem to keep her downstairs."

Her hollow-sounding "okay" stuck with him as he walked downstairs. All her replies sounded empty. *Something is wrong here, Lord.* Halfway down the stairs, Peter was impressed with a mental picture of a young puppy, whimpering and bleeding. *God, are You telling me she's badly hurt?*

◇◇◇◇◇◇◇◇◇◇◇◇◇◇◇

"Oh, Amber. Good timin'!" Faye carried a towel-covered basket to the table set for four people.

"Here, Amber." Peter held out a chair for her near the French doors leading out to a deck swept mostly clean of snow. He watched her glance toward the fireplace then warily eye a reclining Sassy before crossing toward him. As she sat down, he gently pushed her chair forward then walked over to help his mom carry the pot of beef stew from the kitchen.

"Hmmm. Smells great, love!" Frank walked into the dining room and kissed his wife on the cheek.

"Thank you, dear. Amber, do you like ice in your water or would you rather have some juice?"

"Water is fine."

"I'll get it, Mom. You sit down."

"Oh, thank you, Peter."

Peter filled two glasses with ice water, carrying one to Amber before sitting across from her with his own.

"Okay, let's thank God for this," Frank said, bowing his head and clasping his hands together in front of him.

"Thank You, Father, for the food You've giv'n us and for the added blessing of a new friend. Help us be the blessing You mean us to be and let us enjoy each other in the time we have. Amen."

Peter grabbed the bowl of salad and piled some on his plate before passing it to his mom.

"Where are you from, Amber?" Faye asked as she passed biscuits around.

"California."

"Does your family live down there?"

Amber shrugged in response to Faye's question. "I don't know."

Peter stopped mid-bite and looked earnestly at Amber. *She doesn't know if her family lives in California?* His mind reeled. He watched as Amber pulled off a small piece of her biscuit and dipped it into her stew.

Peter met his mother's eyes then glanced at his father. *This conversation needs a new direction. Quickly.* "How was Micah today, Dad?"

Peter watched Amber close her eyes and breathe deeply.

"Makin' it through."

"Peter, will you please hand me the honey?" said Faye.

"He's havin' a tough time, 'course, but he's still openin' up the store every day," said Frank.

"Did you mention coming out to dinner to him?" asked Faye.

"Yeah. He said maybe in a couple weeks. Oops." Some beef stew dropped onto the red tablecloth embroidered with white snowflakes. "Sorry 'bout that, love. Micah said he'd call the office when the saw blades are in. You can prob'ly corner him into a day then." Frank winked lovingly at his wife.

Peter knew that Faye could talk anyone into dinner when she set her mind to it. Micah would be over to eat at least once before Christmas, if not for Thanksgiving as well.

Amber's probably lost in all this local talk. "Micah lost his wife this past summer," Peter said to her. "The weeks between Thanksgiving and Christmas were her favorite time of year, so Mom's worried Micah is taking the season hard."

Amber nodded in acknowledgement but remained silent.

"Well, he's not called about a tree and Allie said he hardly leaves the house except to go to the store."

Peter continued gently. "Yes, Mom, I know. But I think Micah's entitled to a bit of a hard Christmas. Imagine how different this year must be for him."

"That doesn't mean we have to leave him sitting at home every night, Peter. He can mourn his loss, but we can't let him sit and mope all Christmas. God is still good, even when He takes things we love away."

Peter ate silently for a few moments. *I understand what Mom's saying, God, but would I act any different from Micah? How long would it take me to move on? How do you show hope in the eternal in the midst of the pain of the temporal?*

"Speakin' of God's goodness, did you hear that Chad and Amy are expectin' again?"

"Oh, Frank! How wonderful! When did you find out?"

"Chad stopped me before I headed into town earlier. Hand me another biscuit, son."

Peter held the basket out to his dad. He started to offer one to Amber when he noticed she still had about half of a biscuit. She took a tentative bite of stew from her half-full bowl.

"Hmm. These have to be the finest biscuits you've made in a while, love." Frank ripped his bread into pieces and added it to his stew. "Chad said Amy's been a might ill. And little Joshua's caught himself the flu."

"Oh, goodness. I'll make a batch of chicken noodle soup for them. Peter, will you have time to deliver it to them tomorrow if I get it done first thing in the morning?"

Peter thought about his schedule while chewing. Fridays were normally pretty light for him, but with Thanksgiving the next week and trees needed on the Christmas tree lot the day after, his days were busier. "I'll be heading into Portland tomorrow night. I'll leave here around 5:00 and I can drop it off on my way. Will that be soon enough?"

"I'll call Amy and let her know to expect you," said Faye. "Are you going to be late tomorrow?"

Peter rinsed down a bite with a gulp of water and considered his mom's question. He knew she didn't particularly care for his weekly trips to the city but she tried hard not to interfere. "I don't think I'll be too late, Mom. Stephanie and I have a dinner reservation at the restaurant in her building at 6:30 but no plans after that."

"Well, tell her we said hello when you see her. I expect she's got plans for Thanksgiving next week."

"Yeah. She's committed to working at the parade in the morning, then a benefit later that night. It sounded like she'd be pretty well tied up all day."

"Did ya mention the party in December to her?" said Frank.

"Yeah, Dad. She said she'd check her schedule but I'm pretty sure she's coming." *Why does it always feel like I'm making excuses for her?*

"Are you going to have a chance to see your sister before next week?" said Frank.

"I don't think so, Dad. What do you need Brittney for?"

"Just lookin' for some ice cream for Thanksgivin' is all."

Faye put her napkin down and looked at her husband. "Frank, really. Don't bother Brittney. I can get some at the grocery store."

"It's not the good stuff," said Frank.

"It's the same brand," said Faye.

Frank grunted as he wiped his bowl with a piece of biscuit.

Faye scooted her chair back and stood, grabbing her dishes and walking toward the sink.

Peter followed his mom to the sink with his own dishes. "I can drive by the creamery tomorrow, Dad, but I think they'll be closed."

"Don't worry about it, son." His eyes twinkled as he looked across the room at Faye. "I'm sure I can survive on whatever your mom brings home."

Peter chuckled. His dad's wink told him that Brittney would be getting a phone call before Thursday. "How 'bout I get some more wood brought in, then we finish up that game of chess from last night?"

"Sounds good. I think I figured me a way to get you on the defense."

Peter chuckled. As he called Sassy to his side and headed to the mudroom he said, "All right. I'll meet you in the living room."

Chapter 3

AFTER DINNER, AMBER SAT NEAR the hearth and soaked up the fire's heat, struggling to remain awake as she listened to the conversation. Still full from the bit of stew she'd managed to eat, she'd turned down Faye's steaming blueberry cobbler with vanilla ice cream. Peter and Frank played chess for about an hour before Faye caught Amber nodding off and sent her to bed.

She gratefully said goodnight to the family and made her way upstairs. As she entered her room, she found the bedside light turned on, the bed covers neatly turned down, and a book on her pillow. A note attached to the front of the book said,

> *Just in case you like to read.*
> *We're glad you're here, Amber.*
> *Faye*

Amber removed the note and looked at the front cover. *Two Minute Devotions? Great. Just what I need. All my problems solved in two minutes or less.* She tossed the book onto the bedside table.

The next morning Amber glimpsed how important religion was to them. Behind the circular staircase was a room filled with bookshelves. Amber had never before seen so many books in one home. She cautiously approached the area, getting close enough to scan the titles and authors. Some names she recognized, like Billy Graham. *One whole shelf of different Bibles? Why would three people want so many Bibles?*

As she continued browsing the room, she came to a small table beside a beautifully etched wooden rocker. On the table was a box of tissues and a worn, blue leather Bible. In the lower right corner of the front cover, Amber read stamped in gold letters: "To My Beloved." She reached out to carefully touch the letters, lost in the few good memories she had.

"You are welcome to read any of the books in here anytime you like."

Amber jumped at Peter's voice and snatched her hand back from the Bible as she turned to face him. *How long has he been watching?*

"We each have our favorites, but most of them are pretty good. Do you have someone you like read?" Still dressed in jogging clothes and tennis shoes, Peter wiped a bead of sweat from his temple as he waited for her response.

"No." *I wish I could read enough books to be able to choose a favorite!*

"Well, then, what's your favorite kind of book to read?"

Kind of book? Amber stared blankly at Peter, not sure how to answer his question.

"Do you like fiction, history, poetry?"

Amber shifted uneasily from one foot to another. *A guy with a library in his house couldn't possibly understand a lack of books.* "I just read whatever I find laying around."

"We have several fiction books over here." Peter walked to the bookshelf by the large bay window at the front of the house. "Mom likes Beverly Lewis, although Dee Henderson can have a little more action in her books if you like that." He had pulled one off the shelf and held it out to her.

Amber hesitated then moved to take it from him. "Thanks." *Maybe if I look interested in the book, he'll leave me alone.* Problem was, not only did Peter leave like she hoped, his presence left with him.

What is it about him that gets to me? Come on, girl! You can't be getting attached to these people. They aren't worth the cost.

◇×◇×◇×◇×◇×◇×◇×◇×◇×◇×◇

At least the family didn't make a huge deal over church. Saturday afternoon, curled up in the chair closest to the fire to read the book she'd taken from Peter the day before, Frank interrupted her when he came in to add a log to the fire.

"Enjoyin' the book?"

"Hmm? Oh, yes." *Why do people always get chatty when you're reading?*

"Which one ya got?"

Amber flipped to the front cover and showed him the title. "Peter said it was a good action book."

"As I recall, there's a whole series of 'em in there. Peter seemed to like 'em well enough but I'm thinkin' I only read a couple. But then I ain't much into fiction. You help yourself to any of those books. That's what they're there for."

"Thank you." Amber opened the book, eager to get back to the story.

Frank walked to the end of the couch and looked back at her. "I don't know how exactly you feel 'bout this, but we attend church services on Sunday mornin's. You're always welcome to join us. We leave 'bout nine."

Amber wasn't quite sure how to respond. Church folks never seemed to like her and she'd never found much use for them. *But after giving me a job and a place to sleep, how do I tell him no?*

Thankfully, Frank didn't really seem to expect an answer. He was already heading toward the garage.

Faye was just as easy Sunday morning over breakfast. Amber came downstairs to the smell of fresh muffins. She breathed deeply as she approached the kitchen. "That smells really good," she said.

"Why, thank you, Amber. Have a seat on one of those bar stools there while I get the butter and jellies." Faye handed Amber a basket overflowing with large muffins still warm from the oven. "Hot muffins just sounded so good this morning, and they make for a quick cleanup before church. Would you like some milk or some juice?"

"Milk, please."

"You know, you are always welcome to join us for church."

Amber's stomach turned. "I appreciate that." Not wanting to make eye contact with Faye, she busied herself adding some butter to her strawberry muffin.

Faye sat down beside her, placing a glass of milk near her plate. "You know, I didn't always like church." She patted Amber's knee before continuing. "In fact, I didn't really start going regular until just before Frank and I got married. It was important to him, you see, but I'd never had much use for it. It just wasn't important to my parents when I was growing up."

Amber listened attentively but still couldn't bring herself to look Faye in the eyes.

"Amber, what I'm trying to say is that it's okay if you don't want to go with us this morning. Many people have been hurt by church-goin' folks. Others just don't see a need to go to services. Whatever your reasons, if you ever change your mind, just know that you're welcome. Okay?"

Amber looked at Faye for just a moment, unsure what to say. "Thank you."

"Now then, if you'd like to do some laundry, just help yourself. The washer and dryer are right back through that door." Faye pointed to a door just to the right of the sink. "And I'll ask Peter to stoke up the fire real good so you can sit and read in the living room if you'd like. You just make yourself at home."

As Faye rambled on about when she thought they'd be back and various plans for the week, Amber's mind continued to wrestle with the same question she'd had from the start: *Is this family for real?* Her thoughts circled around the family, analyzing their behaviors and possible hidden motives. Hope continually fought to spring to life, but in her experience people just weren't kind. Kindness always had strings attached and the only way to survive was to figure out what the person really wanted before you got emotionally tied. It was easier to walk away with the person's dark side exposed. *It's easier to walk away. . . .*

As Amber lay in bed Monday morning and reviewed her weekend, she continued to struggle to find any ulterior motives. The family seemed genuinely nice. Faye had really made soup for the family who was sick and Peter had really left with it the next evening. The few employees she'd met on Friday all seemed pleasant and showed affection for Faye and admiration for Frank. And the family had left without her for church on Sunday morning without a hint of condemnation.

Peter unnerved her, though. He easily stood eight or nine inches taller than her short stature and at least sixty pounds heavier. He obviously ran consistently and his arms boasted muscles used to working in the Oregon forest. His hair was slightly darker than her own brown locks and his mouth always seemed ready to smile. But his eyes were what caught her breath. She'd always considered her eyes to be boring and expressionless, mousy brown like her hair, but his blue eyes pierced through her until she felt like she was standing emotionally naked in front of him. *How much does he really see?*

At least Sassy usually gave her a reason to avoid him. She and the dog had come to a wary alliance, at least on Amber's part. Amber preferred it if the dog kept her distance but Sassy seemed to like her. *Figures. The one I most fear is the one who wants to stick closest.*

Amber rolled over and looked at the clock. *7:24.* She gave a stretch before getting out of bed. If she got moving she could get done in the shower and back to her own room before Peter came upstairs.

<><><><><><><><><><><>

Thanksgiving was important to Faye. Amber struggled to keep up as they went through the grocery store with a list that seemed long enough to feed a dozen families. If she understood right, this was going to be her first major gathering at the Yager home. Peter's older brother, Logan, and his wife, Heather, would be coming along with their three children, as well as his younger sister, Brittney, and Frank's dad, whom everyone called Pops. Faye also called to invite Chad, who was like Frank's son, along with his wife and their two boys, plus Micah and his son Andy and Andy's wife, Allie.

I wish I'd showed up a week later! She sighed quietly as Faye put some green beans into the cart and looked over her list. *Maybe I'll finally learn what these people are all about. Family tends to bring out darker sides.*

"Oh, Amber!" Faye said. "I forgot the marshmallows. Will you please go back and get some? I need a bag of the little ones— Frank likes them baked over the sweet potatoes. And I also need a bag of the big ones for cooking over the fire later in the evening. Thank you!"

Amber dutifully went back through the store looking for marshmallows, sighing as she tried to remember where she had seen them. *Later in the evening? Didn't she say Brittney and Pops would be there by 9:00 a.m. for cinnamon rolls? It sounds like people will be filling the house all day! Ugh!*

Lost in her thoughts, she almost ran straight into Peter. "Oh!" She tried to back up quickly while Peter reached to steady her. "Sorry."

"Dad sent the cavalry. He thought you might need backup to get all of Mom's Thanksgiving purchases home."

Amber grinned as she thought back to the two full grocery carts she'd just left with Faye and their Camry's back seat full of mums. "I was beginning to wonder how we'd fit everything into her car."

"You look lost. Did Mom send you back for something?" Peter's eyes sparkled.

"Marshmallows. She said the little ones for sweet potatoes and the big ones for roasting over a fire."

"Ah, yes," Peter nodded. "Dad's sweet tooth and Logan's kids." Peter began leading the way to an aisle near the produce with all the baking supplies. "The only way Dad will touch a sweet potato is if it is smothered in marshmallows. And Logan's kids will think something is horribly wrong if there are no s'mores Thanksgiving afternoon."

"S'mores?"

"Mmm. Chocolate, roasted marshmallow, graham cracker. Sound familiar?"

"No. This is a popular treat around here?" Amber's mouth was watering at the idea of such a concoction. Her mind held a faint memory of roasted marshmallows. *Surely chocolate would just make it better.*

Peter stopped in front of the stock of marshmallows and stared at Amber. "You've never had a s'more? Your family must not have been into camping."

"Uh, no." Amber started to add more. Part of her longed to trust Peter, but history hadn't been kind. Thankfully Peter didn't seem to notice.

"Well, then, you are in for a treat! If your appetite for Mom's fudge pie last night is any indication, you're gonna love s'mores!"

Chapter 4

"OKAY, MOM," PETER SAID AS he closed the trunk of his mom's black Camry. "That's the last bag. Now you go get in my Jeep with Amber and head on home. I've got to stop over at Micah's then I'll be right behind you."

"Are you sure you don't mind, Peter? I can take the car home."

"I know you can, Mom, but I'd prefer you drive the Jeep. The fresh snow makes a couple of those turns on the road home tricky and the Jeep has better traction."

"All right, then. Please don't be long. I want to get these groceries unloaded and organized so I can start working on the desserts."

"Yes, ma'am. I should only be at Micah's about five minutes."

Peter watched his mom get into the driver's seat of his Jeep. As they pulled out, he saw Amber look his way but jerk back as soon as they made eye contact.

Father, I don't know about this girl you sent us, Peter prayed. *She frustrates me! Just when I think she's going to trust me with some bit of information, she clams up again. What was that look over the marshmallows about?*

Nothing. Apparently God was keeping His information as close as Amber was keeping her thoughts.

Peter breathed in deeply as he got into his mother's car and turned toward Micah's Hardware. *Jesus, we need help with her. Did I hand her the right book to read the other morning? She seems to enjoy it. But is it making a difference? Father, don't let her leave us farther from You than she was when she arrived. Use us to draw her in.*

◇◇◇◇◇◇◇◇◇◇◇◇◇◇◇◇◇◇◇

"Hey, Micah!"

"Peter! Good to see you." Micah put down the screwdrivers he was organizing and stood to his full six-foot height to shake Peter's hand.

"Got some new stock in?" Peter raised his eyebrows slightly and nodded toward the screwdrivers Micah had just been sorting.

"Nah. Chad was just in here with Josh and Caleb. Those two boys love these tools and I didn't have the heart to get after them today."

"Things going okay with Amy?" Peter was suddenly concerned. He'd meant to ask Chad yesterday how Amy and the boys were, but the day got away from him in the wood shop and he'd never gone down to the logging garage to find him.

"Oh, yeah. She's still got some morning sickness, but Chad says things are better now that Joshua's back to normal. Thankfully Caleb never caught it."

"Good. Hey, Amber said you called to tell us the blades for the band saw were in."

"Sure are. I figured you'd be in to get them today or tomorrow, so I put them right back here." Micah walked behind the front counter and opened a cabinet. "How's that girl working out?"

"She's quiet. Definitely been hurt. But she picks things up fast and does whatever Mom asks her to do."

"Sometimes I wonder at your dad and how he takes in every wounded creature he finds." Micah stood and placed the new blades on the counter.

"Well, sometimes Jesus went to the sick and sometimes they came to Him. Dad's always figured that God knew where he was and where he planned to be. All he had to do was keep his heart ready to minister and God would provide the opportunities."

"I hope this time works out for you guys."

Peter grabbed the package of blades, quickly asking God for wisdom. "You know, Micah, people can be tough to love. Despite our best efforts, sometimes they choose to walk away from those that can most help." Peter looked intently into Micah's eyes. "But even when people make the worst possible decisions, God still considers them worth the effort to love."

Micah firmed his jaw. His eyes watered slightly as the quiet throughout the store expanded for a long moment. As he quietly nodded, Micah said, "You tell that mother of yours that I'll be seeing her for Thanksgiving."

"I will, Micah. See you Thursday."

∞∞∞∞∞∞∞∞∞∞∞∞

"Things should turn out nicely this year."

Peter could see how pleased his mom was. She loved having people over, but parties were her specialty.

"Amber, dear, you start putting all the baking supplies on the table so we can organize them by recipe. I'll work on getting all the cold stuff put into the refrigerator and, Peter, will you please work on putting everything else away for me?"

It was only Monday afternoon, but by tomorrow night, Peter knew the house would be filled with the smells of Thanksgiving desserts.

"Oh, Peter, will you plug in the extra fridge so it's cold and ready for me to use tomorrow, please?"

"Already done, Mom. I plugged it in before I headed into town this morning."

"Wonderful! Now, help me think where everyone's going to sit. Let's see. My last count included thirteen adults and five children. We'll use the high chair for Megan, which leaves us with two two-year-olds and two four-year-olds. If we put the other two chairs at the dining room table, that will seat eight of us."

Peter paused in organizing the can goods to look critically at the dining area. "What if we turned the table sideways, then added the folded table to the other side, doubling the width of the dining table? It might be a little tight around the wall and glass doors, but we should be able to fit ten or eleven around there plus the highchair. If we lay a blanket on the floor over by the staircase, Logan and I can have a picnic with the kids."

"Can you bring those wooden chairs up from the office Wednesday afternoon?"

"Sure. I can—"

"Oh! Peter!" Faye shut the freezer with a quick slam and walked over to the dining table where Amber was diligently organizing sugar, chocolate, and berries. "Do you think we can fit two of those folded tables here?"

Peter walked over and eyed the space. "Probably, Mom. What are you thinking?"

"Allie just bought a table like ours for organizing the end of year tax paperwork. If we brought the bench up from the shop for the little ones . . ."

"Hmm. Just might work, Mom. The back legs on that bench need tightening up, but I should be able to get to that before Thursday."

"Wonderful!" Faye gave Amber a quick squeeze. "This is just wonderful! In just three short days our home will be full of all my favorite people!"

Peter couldn't help but watch Amber during his mother's outburst of excitement. She certainly wasn't returning the loving embrace but she also didn't seem as tense as she had the first couple of days.

Good, thought Peter as he went back to sorting non-perishables for the pantry. *Someone in this family seems to be making her feel at ease!*

∞∞∞∞∞∞∞∞∞∞

Peter breathed deeply as he shut the door behind him. In many ways, the wood shop was his sanctuary. He loved the smell of the wood as he worked with it. In his youth he had marveled at the trees God created: the Douglas fir, regally stretching into the sky and perfect for beams and trusses; the western red cedar, beautiful both in nature and in paneling for homes; the red alder, gorgeous in the autumn and precious as a carved toy in the hands of a child. *So much variety, Father, in height and in purpose. Thank You for the trees and for the love You gave me for them.*

Peter walked over to the old bench he'd moved down from outside the logging office. Six feet long, the white oak wood had been rubbed smooth with years of use.

So much laughter has been shared on this bench, so much counsel given, Father. Help us to continue to use this wood for Your glory. Peter lifted the bench onto the worktable so he could check out the leg joints. He grabbed some wood glue and a screwdriver off nearby shelves.

Let this bench be a gathering place for many more years, as men take time to sit together and share their lives. Let it be not only a place where men come together, but a place where men are drawn closer to You.

Peter set the bench aside to dry and walked over to his project area. His mother's Christmas present was coming along nicely. He'd been working for the last few weeks on something she could sit on while enjoying her favorite spot down at the river. It was inspired by the rough-looking log furniture but with a smooth back for his mom's comfort and big enough for his dad to join her.

Peter grabbed his small chisel and carefully began working on the verse he was carving into the back: *The LORD has chosen you to be his treasured possession,* from Deuteronomy 14:2.

Father, as she rests on this bench, cement this verse into my mother's heart. Use her to teach others this same truth. Never let her fall into the thinking that she is too old to be useful but continue to guard her mind and clearly show her the part of Your plan that You want her to fulfill. Protect her so that she may be free from further pain and grant her supernatural wisdom so that she would give the women You bring her godly counsel.

At this Peter thought of Amber and paused in his work. *She's a tough one, Father.*

Yes. Peter could almost hear the Holy Spirit responding back to him.

There must be hope for You to have brought her here.

Of course.

But what do we do? How do we reach her? I can see slight differences in the way she responds to Mom, but she's got such thick walls up.

Love her.

Love her. Peter sighed. *I know that's always the answer. But how do we love her? Whatever happened caused deep wounds.*

Yes.

How do we fix wounds we can't see and she won't talk about?

Love her.

Peter paused in his work. His eyes focused on the words from Deuteronomy: *treasured possession. How do we convince Amber that she is one of Your treasured possessions?*

Silence.

Peter sighed. "Perfect," Peter muttered as he rose from the bench. *Love. So simple, yet so complicated.* "It's a great time for You to get quiet on me." Peter looked heavenward, not really expecting a reply. Usually the silence meant the answer was staring him in the face. He just had to figure it out.

Chapter 5

FAYE WATCHED OUT THE DINING room window as Peter locked up the wood shop and headed toward the river. She'd found him lost in thought more than once in the last few days. *Deep in thought. Or in prayer.* She wasn't sure which. But it wasn't quite like him. He was definitely puzzling over something. "That's not the path he normally walks, Lord. In fact. . . . Hmm. Now isn't that interesting." Peter hadn't followed that path in several months. "Very interesting."

Chapter 6

AMBER WOKE EARLY THURSDAY MORNING and breathed deeply. *Mmmm. More yummy smells from downstairs.*

Thanksgiving preparations had consumed Faye all week. Amber quickly learned that Monday was shopping day, Tuesday was pie day, Wednesday was bread day, and Thursday was dinner day.

She stretched her tired muscles as she remembered all the work she and Faye had done together. With Faye's patient guidance, Amber mixed and rolled out four pie crusts, preparing them for the fillings: pumpkin, black cherry, mountain huckleberry, and lemon piled high with a softly browned meringue. *I remember meringue like that.*

Before she got teary eyed, Amber threw back the covers and crawled out of bed. Her back and arm muscles complained from the workout they had received the day before kneading dough. For Thanksgiving breakfast, Faye insisted on cinnamon sourdough bread as well as homemade cinnamon rolls. There was also fresh-baked wheat bread available, *and do I smell muffins?* Amber's belly grumbled in response.

She had also helped Faye prepare yeast rolls for the Thanksgiving dinner—enough for everyone to have at least two, plus several larger ones for those who wanted turkey sandwiches later on in the evening or the next day for lunch.

I'd better stop thinking about what's done and get ready for what's coming. After wincing through one more stretch, Amber grabbed a pair of jeans, a navy blue T-shirt, and a blue and green plaid shirt before heading to the door. After checking the clock one final time to make sure Peter would still be out running, she opened the door and almost screamed.

"Sassy! What are you doing here?"

Dark chocolate eyes looked at her as Sassy lay directly in her path. The brown face with its white stripe down the middle was beginning to grow on her.

"I suppose you are kinda cute. For a dog."

Sassy tilted her head slightly to the right and raised her eyebrows.

"Don't take that to mean I like you! Now go on. Go find someone else."

Sassy tilted her head to the left.

"Wait a minute! Why aren't you out with—"

"Sassy!" Peter appeared at the top of the stairs. Amber clutched her clothes tightly to her, frozen in position. Suddenly, her knee-length flannel nightgown didn't seem like nearly enough covering.

"Amber, I'm sorry. Sassy, come here." The dog obediently got up and went to Peter's side. "I find her sleeping at your door just about every morning. Andy and I decided to take this morning off running. I'll get her out of here right away." Peter turned to head back downstairs without looking at her again.

"Come on, Sass."

Sassy looked back at Amber.

"Sassy! Now!"

Peter sounded rushed. *Anxious maybe. Stressed? Odd.*

Amber shook her long hair and proceeded to the bathroom. She turned on the water to get hot, then undressed and stopped to look in the mirror. *Definitely some changes going on here. Faye's cooking is doing my ribs some good and my hair's looking better. It would be so easy to get used to hot showers and Faye's company.* Amber sighed, turning away from her reflection to get into the water.

◇◇◇◇◇◇◇◇◇◇◇◇◇◇◇◇◇◇◇◇◇◇

"Hey, Mom!"

"Brittney, dear! Good morning!"

Amber stopped mid-bite into her cinnamon roll to see a dark-haired woman burst into the kitchen. Not quite as tall as Peter, the slim woman dressed in jeans and an Oregon Health & Science University hoodie plopped three bags down onto the floor so she could embrace Faye.

"Where's Pops?" said Faye.

Brittney waved a hand in the air. "Oh, you know Pops! He's got Peter chasing down some vibration he heard in my engine on the drive here. I tried to convince him the Chevy dealer looked it over just a week ago, but you know him! I'll just go put these—oh! I'm sorry. Mom, why didn't you tell me we had company already?"

"Brittney, this here's Amber, the one I told you has been so helpful!"

"Hi, Amber. It's great to meet you."

Amber smiled meekly.

"Mom's been raving about you all week!" said Brittney.

"What kind of ice cream did you get?" said Faye.

"You know that I made a trip to Tillamook Ice Creamery for Dad. I'll put them in the outside freezer for later. Those cinnamon rolls smell wonderful! I'm ready to dig in!"

Amber sighed. *It's going to be a long day.*

∞◇∞◇∞◇∞◇∞◇∞◇∞

"S'more?"

"Hmm?" Amber picked her head up off the back of the chair and looked at Peter. She was contently nestled in the leather chair by the fire, even though Sassy lay on the floor beneath her.

Peter flashed his crooked smile. "I asked if you wanted a s'more. Here."

Amber took the small plate from him and looked at the concoction. Marshmallow oozed on all sides of the graham cracker. "Umm, exactly how am I supposed to eat this?"

Peter sat down on the ottoman in front of her. "Don't worry. No one 'round here can do it neatly."

There's that crooked smile again. As she tried her best to pick up the snack at the neatest possible corner, she realized Peter still watched her. "Where's yours?"

"Pops is cooking more. Emma and Taylor are currently gooey messes, and I stole this one while Britt and Logan were wrestling for it."

Amber had watched the family closely, looking for any signs that what she'd been part of this past week was all a facade. Instead she'd been confronted with a lot of laughter. Best she could tell, Logan was three or four years older than Peter, and Brittney was about that much younger. But they interacted like they depended on each other. Like they enjoyed depending on each other.

Even more confusing was that Logan's wife, Heather, didn't seem like she was any less part of the family. Faye looked after her as much as she did Brittney, and Heather moved comfortably about the kitchen like she was in her own home. And Micah's daughter-in-law, Allie, was openly accepted too, like she belonged.

It's only natural that the grandkids are loved by everyone, thought Amber. At four and two, Emma's and Taylor's blonde hair, blue eyes, and chubby cheeks would easily win over most adults. And six-month-old Megan's smile was irresistible. *But that doesn't explain Chad's boys.*

To say Chad and Amy's boys were a handful was an understatement, but no one seemed to mind. More than once Amber watched Peter, Logan, or Andy grab one or the other of Chad's sons to wrestle, throw in the snow, or otherwise divert some energy.

Maybe there isn't anything more to find here but the love written about in books. She sighed.

"What are you thinking about?"

Amber suddenly became aware that Peter was still on the ottoman near her. She stared at him for a moment, not sure what she could safely tell him about her thoughts.

"Seemed like a lot of meaning in that sigh," said Peter.

Just at that moment Heather came marching through the French doors holding four-year-old Emma as far from her as she possibly could. Emma's face was streaked with chocolate and her blonde hair boasted several puffs of marshmallow. Her tongue was still working hard to clean whatever it could get off her chubby fingers before Mom got to the tub.

"One day I'll miss this, right?" Heather said, giggling as she rushed through the living room and into the bathroom.

Amber couldn't help a chuckle. Sassy thumped her tail in response.

"We didn't overwhelm you today, did we?" said Peter. "Mom likes a lot of people for her holiday gatherings."

Amber looked down at the s'more, appreciating the change of subject. "No. It was okay." She was still trying to figure out a good place to bite without ending up like Emma. "You have a nice family, Peter."

"Yeah. It hasn't always been easy." Peter seemed lost in thought for a moment.

Amber waited on him to continue, deciding to try small bites of the s'more. *How much could he possibly know about hard times?*

"Still, I'm thankful for the family we have. I can't imagine life without my brother and sister around, not that I always appreciate them being close. And Pops certainly knows how to keep things interesting."

"Sounds like there are some good stories in your grandfather's past." Amber put the s'more down for a moment to see if she could lick the mess off her fingers before it got out of hand.

"Pops is the oldest of five kids, and he takes family very seriously. He's protective, almost like a lion in charge of his pride. But he also tends to, shall we say, instigate things."

"Instigate?"

"When we were younger, he was constantly pranking us. Snake skins in our shoes, frogs in our beds, quarters glued onto the porch." Peter chuckled.

"One time when Britt was getting ready to go out with friends, he turned off the hot water supply right in the middle of her shower." Amber watched a sparkle appear in Peter's eyes.

"Was she furious?"

"Probably. But Britt isn't one to take things like that lying down." Peter chuckled again. "She doesn't show her anger. She strikes back. She came out of the bathroom without giving any hint that something was wrong. Her friends showed up and she sweetly kissed Pops on the cheek as she headed out the door."

"That wasn't the end of it?"

"At first we thought it was. We were all pretty disappointed, especially Pops. Logan and I were certain she'd come flying out of that bathroom swinging at all of us until she figured out which one was guilty. But somehow she knew, or at least guessed right." Peter could barely contain his laughter as he retold the story.

"What happened?"

"Well, when Pops decided to go home, his car wouldn't start. He worked on it for several minutes before he thought to look in the right place. Before Britt left to go out with her friends, she'd removed the coil wire in his engine and took it with her! He couldn't go anywhere until she returned home."

"How'd she know to remove that?"

"Pops is big on cars. He's always insisted that before we could own a car, we had to know how to care for it. We've all been helping him on various engines and machinery around here most our lives."

Although Peter was enjoying the memories, Amber couldn't begin to imagine her own family acting like this. *Dad would have been furious and everyone within shouting distance would have known it! And Cassie . . . oh! Cassie.* Amber felt her eyes burning as she struggled to get her brain to think of something besides her sister. Anything besides Cassie.

Sassy stretched out beneath Amber's feet. *Yes! Thank you, Sassy!* "So, Andy runs with you and Sassy in the mornings?"

Peter looked at her, his eyes squinting in the outer corners for a moment.

"Yeah. Andy and I basically grew up together. Dad met Micah when we first moved out here soon after Logan was born. Mom and Micah's wife, Helen, became great friends. Andy was born just a couple months after me, so we were in the same classes at school. We've just always stuck together."

Amber was certain Peter suspected she'd purposely changed the subject, but thankfully he didn't ask her about it.

"Who was your closest friend growing up?" said Peter.

Amber looked behind Peter's left shoulder as she thought back to her childhood. "Well, there was one girl who lived on our street when I was little. Michelle. No, Melissa. Hmm. Something like that. We liked to play dolls." Just mentioning her old friend caused a ping to her heart. *How did we go from one touchy subject to another?*

Peter's eyes narrowed again. "Did she move away?"

Amber nibbled on her bottom lip, trying to think of some way to get out of this conversation. "No." She focused her eyes on her s'more, not that she could stomach another bite of what had been chocolaty heaven just moments before. "Things happened and we couldn't be friends anymore. Then I moved away and that was the end of it."

"Sounds tough."

"Yeah." Amber shrugged, desperately trying to sound nonchalant. "Life goes on."

"Have you not had anyone close to you since then?" Peter's gentle prying wasn't helping her control the emotions bubbling to the surface.

"Not really. I don't tend to stay in one place for long and I never write. Makes it hard to keep friends."

Peter was so quiet that she braved a look at him. He leaned toward her, his arms on his knees, patiently waiting. *What is that in his eyes? Sympathy? Pity?* At first anger rose inside her. *How dare he judge my life that way!* But something about his look made her stop. *Peter is the fortunate one. He has a world of people who love him.* Amber's eyes began filling with tears. She was dangerously close to crying. *I've got to get out of here.*

She began to look for something, anything, to use to extract herself from the situation. *Surely Emma is done in the bathtub, or Faye needs more ice cream from the garage, or Pops needs help instigating.*

A sudden commotion of laughter at the dining room French doors caught Peter's attention. Amber thrust the s'more into Peter's hands and scrambled out of the chair, almost tripping over Sassy. She ran upstairs, trying hard not to slam the bathroom door behind her.

Chapter 7

"How're things going with Amber?"

"What's that supposed to mean?" Peter stopped mid-stride on the path they normally took through Cascade Mountains and turned to face Andy.

"Whoa, buddy." Andy put his hands up before his chest. "You lookin' to fight this morning? I'd rather not start something but if something's on your heart let's get it out and deal with it."

Peter wasn't quite sure how to answer him. They'd finished their jog for the morning and were cooling down with a walk, but he knew his temper was short. At only about an inch shorter than himself, Andy was Peter's match in speed and muscle. But he knew deep down that a fight with Andy wouldn't solve anything. Amber irritated him. Or maybe, more accurately, God was irritating him.

"Things are . . . going."

"She seemed comfortable with your mom when we were there for Thanksgiving yesterday."

"Yeah." Peter sighed. "She is definitely more relaxed around Mom than she was at first. And she's still reading that book. I just . . . I don't know." He ran his hand through his hair. "I'm struggling to maintain perspective."

"What kind of perspective?" The guys stopped as they reached their jeeps and grabbed water bottles, each drinking a sizeable portion.

"Well, Andy, I don't quite know how to explain it. I feel drawn to her, but she's not saved. Every time I pray about how to help her, God either remains silent or He simply says 'love her.' But how do I accomplish that without scaring her away, giving her false hope, or hurting both of us?"

"Well, let's think about this for a moment."

Peter most appreciated his friend's natural ability to cut to core issues when his own head spun in circular arguments. Andy had a gift for asking just the right question, which aided him in his career as Crossing's lawyer and always seemed to help Peter refocus on the task at hand.

"Okay. God specifically told you to 'love her'?"

"Yes."

"Well, there are many ways to love, different types of love, but they all involve the heart. So, how deeply can you allow her to touch your heart?"

"Exactly."

"Hmm. With the anger I saw a moment ago, maybe a better question is how deeply do you *want* her to touch your heart?"

"I can't even think like that, Andy!"

"You can't, or won't?"

Peter ran his hands through his hair again, frustrated at the question. "I can't allow myself to think that way. She's not saved. She's shown no interest in a relationship with God. I can't allow myself to walk down a road which will force my heart to choose between my God and a woman I love."

"I get that. But, what if God is using you to help draw her? If God said 'love her,' then He's asking you to enter into some kind of relationship with her. It sounds like the real battle in your heart is the difference between the relationship you'd like to have and the one you think may be required of you."

Peter rolled his eyes. "Is that supposed to be helpful?"

"Look, you know I only want God's best for you. I don't want you to involve your heart any more than God wants you to, and I certainly don't want your head in the clouds thinking you can change her by loving her."

"So how do I find a balance?" said Peter. "Where is the line between obeying what I know God told me to do, and maybe hurting us both? Whatever happened to her, Andy, she's hurt. Bad. She doesn't even have friends! How can I allow myself to begin to hope that she will trust me enough for something deeper?"

Peter and Andy stared at each other for a long moment before Peter turned to look at the mountains. "As much as part of me longs to obey God, I don't . . ." Peter squared his jaw. "I don't know if I can do this. I'm not sure I want to try."

Andy came up beside Peter, putting a hand on his shoulder. "I can imagine Abraham saying the same thing as he led Isaac up the mountain. He had faith to tell his servant that he and the boy would return, but did his faith waver with the climb? As he built the altar? As he lay his son down?" Andy moved in front of Peter and looked him in the eye. "Pete, I can't tell you what exactly God is asking you to do, but I do know that He treasures obedience. I can pray with you and for Amber, and I'll gladly help keep you accountable. But I challenge you: obey."

Peter sighed deeply, looking at the ground. Andy's hand still lay on his shoulder. Silently he cried out, *Daddy! I just don't know.*

Peter. Those who hope in the Lord . . .

Yes, God. Those who hope in the Lord will renew their strength.

Peter looked up at Andy. "Okay. Obedience it is. Can we pray before heading back?"

"Can't think of a better plan," said Andy. "You want to start?"

Both men bowed their heads as Peter began to pray. "God, I'm not sure I like this path You've placed before me . . ."

◇◇◇◇◇◇◇◇◇◇◇◇◇◇◇◇◇◇

Peter opened the door slightly and kicked snow off his boots before entering the office Monday afternoon. He briefly glanced around then walked across the room toward his mother, noting Amber faced his direction but didn't look his way.

"Here's the updated inventory, Mom. Chad and Jack are loaded down with the logs to fill Harding's order, and a fresh supply of Christmas trees are already loaded on the truck and headed into town."

"Good. Thank you." She took the forms from him and reached for her notebook. He smiled as he remembered their annual trip to Portland to catch the school sales and purchase notebooks, pens, and other office supplies for cheaper than they could get them any other time of year.

"You received two phone calls. Micah called. He forgot to ask you if you needed more sanding belts. His supplier is running a two-day Christmas sale later this week. And Stephanie called. She said dinner Saturday would have to be postponed at least one hour. Something about a hair dresser disaster. Or maybe a dress disaster. I'm not really sure. I'm afraid I got a bit mixed up as she was telling me the problem. Anyway, she said to come for her at 7:30."

Peter stifled a sigh and ignored his mother's not-so-obvious look that begged him to invite her to comment further on Stephanie's call. *Best to avoid that topic.* "Thanks, Mom. I'll check the supply of belts and give Micah a call in the morning."

"Amber, Frank is going to be a tad late for dinner tonight. Why don't you meander on down to the clearing by the river I was telling you about? I'm just going to clean up here and then head back to the house."

"Yes, ma'am. A walk would be nice."

Peter watched her neatly stack the papers then slip over to the coat rack. As he looked more closely, he noticed the seams on her jacket were fraying and more than one spot had been patched with odd pieces of cloth.

Father, thank You for stopping her from traveling farther into the mountains during the winter. That coat's not fit for the journey!

As Peter prayed, his mom stood up and grabbed her own coat.

"Here, dear, borrow my coat for the walk. The frost on those windows tells me the temperature has dropped this afternoon, and I don't want any of us snifflin' around Christmas."

Bless you, Mom!

Peter watched Amber hesitate then gently take the coat. She looked at Faye, murmuring her appreciation.

"Peter, why don't you go with her? You know how tricky those pathways can be. I don't want Amber wandering around lost in the snow!" She gave him a quick shove, neatly pushing him into a position where he found it difficult to refuse.

Amber walked out the door in front of him. She put her hands in the pockets of his mother's coat, waiting for him to point them in the right direction. They walked in silence for a few moments as Peter slowly guided her to his mother's favorite river spot. He wasn't sure whether his mom preferred watching the breathtaking sunsets behind the mountains or listening to the soothing melody of water flowing over rocks downstream.

"Do you like working in the office?"

"Yes."

Peter waited to see if she would add more, but she remained quiet.

"Mom's filing system confuses some of those who help out during the summer."

"It's not that bad," said Amber. She grinned, hinting that she might be covering for his mom a little.

"Are you enjoying the book?"

"Yes. Your dad said that it's a series?"

"Yeah. There's one book for each of the siblings, so six total. Plus there's a book before those that tells the story of Sara."

Amber nodded briefly. "It's good. Giving me a few things to think about."

"Like what?"

"Well, I guess I don't really have a problem with believing there is a God or a supreme being of some kind. But I look at the world and just see pain and chaos. Sure, I might have a few good days in a row, but they never last. Yet this God is supposed to be full of love?"

"A lot of people struggle with that."

"If God really has the power to create this world, and if He truly loves me, then why . . ." Her voice faded.

Peter waited.

"Why is there so much pain? Can He not stop it? Is He powerful enough to make things but not powerful enough to control them? Or does He simply not care about what's going on down here?"

"Those are good questions, ones that a lot of people ask, including Christians. I've worked through them myself, not that I understand everything that happens in and around my family. Does God love me and my family? Yes, I'm confident of it. Even though life's not always easy. God doesn't always make sense. Probably the most difficult situation for me was reconciling God's love with my older sister dying."

"Your older sister died?"

"Yeah. Jamie. She was two years older than me and loved to help Mom in the kitchen. They were always cooking or baking, filling the house with all kinds of smells, mostly good. She was ten years old when she died. She just got sick that spring and never recovered." Peter closed his eyes for a moment, lost in his memory.

"It was probably roughest on Mom. She really struggled for a long time, not wanting to go to church or talk much to her friends. Sometimes she would walk into the kitchen and just cry because Jamie wasn't there with her."

"It's hard to imagine your mom like that."

Peter offered a quick prayer for wisdom. He heard strain in Amber's voice and wondered again about her pain. *Could it be the death of a sibling?*

"It was a couple years before she really began turning things around."

They reached the edge of the river and spent a couple moments in silence. It had been a while since he'd last thought about those awful months after Jamie died. The sounds of the river calmed his spirit.

"Dad said you plan to head further east when the snow melts."

Silence.

"Are you moving closer to family?"

"No," said Amber quietly.

"Then why east?"

"I guess because I've never been there before."

"You are moving just because you've never been there?"

Silence.

"What does your family think?" said Peter.

"I don't know."

"What do you mean, you 'don't know'? Amber, you've said you're not sure where they are. Does your family know anything about your plans?"

"I don't know where my family is and I don't care what they think."

Peter was speechless for a moment. His parents meant the world to him and he couldn't imagine traveling on vacation without their knowledge, much less moving across the country. "I'm not sure what to say, Amber. I don't understand."

"What's to understand? My family isn't like yours. My parents and I just don't get along. I'm better off without them."

"How long have you been on your own, Amber?"

She sighed deeply. "About ten years, I guess."

Ten years? Peter tried not to show too much shock. "How old were you when you left?"

"Sixteen."

"What happened?" The question was barely more than a whisper but the pain he saw deepening in Amber's eyes told Peter she'd heard him. He quietly waited for her answer.

"Amber?"

As he watched her closely, she fought for control, blinking her eyes rapidly. Reaching down to pick up an old stick, she began peeling away pieces of the bark.

"Amber."

She looked at him and held his gaze for a moment.

"I want to help. What happened?"

"Nothing that can be fixed." She looked past him into the forest, then down at the stick that was quickly being shredded. "Nothing that really matters."

"It matters to me."

Her hands stopped working and she closed her eyes. Tears began flowing down her cheeks. Peter closed the distance between them and took her icy hands in his. She jerked back, but he held firm.

"It matters, Amber. Please, tell me."

"Why? Why does this matter? I'll be out of your way in a couple months and you can forget all about me. I'm just a stranger passing through town, no one of any importance that you need concern yourself with."

The speed of her words betrayed her emotions. Peter sensed a tight control she struggled to maintain.

He watched her spin on her heel and take off toward his parents' home. Her tears would not be missed by his mother's sharp eyes and he knew she would offer comfort.

Peter ran his hand through his hair. *If only we knew what was going on!*

Then the Holy Spirit whispered, *"Trust."*

"Who, Father? Her, or me?"

Silence.

"I'll take that to mean both of us," muttered Peter.

Chapter 8

AMBER PEERED INTO THE RESTAURANT mirror before heading back to the lunch table. The week had been quiet after her quick retreat from Peter on Monday, but Faye had taken Friday off to go to Portland to get some Christmas shopping done. She'd encouraged Amber to go with her and, with more fresh snow on the ground, Peter insisted on driving them in his Jeep.

The shopping extravaganza had started at Portland's largest mall then moved on to the upscale mall in downtown. Now they were meeting Brittney for lunch at Romano's Macaroni Grill before moving on to their final stop of the day.

Despite the crowds, shopping with Faye had actually been fun. She had roamed from store to store with purpose, knowing what kinds of gifts she was looking to buy for each person. They had laughed together at one sweater overloaded with sequins and glitter and tested the patience of the chocolatier as they tried multiple samples before choosing which to purchase for Frank.

Peter had dropped them off at doors and called Faye's cell phone periodically to grab packages from them to deposit in the Jeep while intermittently disappearing to do his own shopping.

Now keep it together, girl, Amber chided herself. *You've not had any emotional scenes in four days. Let's keep it that way!* She sighed as she opened the bathroom door and headed back to the table, taking her seat beside Faye. Brittney was suppressing a giggle, eyeing her brother.

"Wherever could it have come from?" She batted her eyelashes at Peter, trying to play innocent, but the gleam in her eyes proved she knew exactly from where "it" had come.

"Stuff it, Britt." Peter couldn't keep his own grin from appearing. "You know full well where the green dye in my shampoo came from."

Amber couldn't hide her shock. *Green dye? In his shampoo?*

"If I hadn't seen it before I put it in my hair, I'd have looked like a pickle for a week."

Brittney couldn't hold her laughter.

"As it was, I had to explain the very elfish-looking tint to my left hand for three days."

Faye giggled. "You two. I cannot imagine where you get it."

"Mother!" Peter and Brittney said in unison. The three burst out laughing, looking from one to the other.

"Well, isn't this quite a scene."

All four heads turned to see who was talking.

"Stephanie. It's good to see you," said Peter.

"Yes, Stephanie," said Faye. "How nice to see you. Are you doing some shopping today?"

Amber took in the fashionably dressed woman from the top of her perfectly combed hair to the tips of her heeled pumps.

"Yes, Faye, I am. The Christmas benefit for Doernbecher Children's Hospital is next week and I need a dress. Will I see you there, Brittney?"

"Oh, I doubt it."

"Oh, goodness. We're being rude!" said Faye. "Amber, this is Stephanie."

"Amber's helping out in the office," said Peter.

"Well, we are a bit far from there, aren't we," said Stephanie.

"Yes, but Amber is proving herself quite capable in a number of areas," said Faye. "This morning would have been stressful without her. I'm very thankful she allowed me to drag her along."

Amber felt the tension rising. Faye's quiet demeanor whenever Stephanie's name came up at home made sense now that she was meeting the woman. Amber didn't return the shrewd looks coming her way, choosing to people watch around the restaurant instead.

"Looks like pizza's here," said Brittney.

"Will you join us?" said Peter. "I can pull up an extra chair."

"No, thank you. I must be going. Still much to accomplish today. Peter, I will see you tomorrow night, correct."

Peter barely nodded his head before Stephanie offered a short farewell and disappeared out of the restaurant almost as quickly as she had appeared.

"Thank goodness skinny buns won't touch greasy food!"

"Britt!"

"Come on, Peter. We both know fancy pants values her model-thin figure too much to dare eat anything as unhealthy as pizza. And as much as I love you, I cannot understand what you see in that woman. She's—"

"Can we change the subject, please?" said Faye. "We are having a splendid day and I refuse to let you two get into a squabble and ruin it. Peter, why don't you offer the blessing so we can eat? I'm starving!"

Amber paused on the stairs and watched Peter arranging gifts under the Christmas tree. He turned to reach for a larger present near the couch and caught her gaze.

"Would you like to help me? I do okay at the shopping and normally pay the store clerks to wrap the boxes, but I can never quite get everything under the tree to Mom's satisfaction."

She smiled. "As many times as I've seen your mom in here the past few days rearranging these presents, I'm not sure I'll do any better than you."

"Then at least come help me so when she does redo them I'll know it's not because I didn't enlist the best help in the house."

Amber descended the last two steps, crossed to the tree, and knelt down to begin making room toward the back for the larger gifts. As she began to take in the full magnitude of the gifts he needed placed around the tree, she asked, "Are all these presents just for your mom and dad?"

"No," said Peter. "The whole family gathers here on Christmas Eve. Logan and Heather will be here with their three kids. And Britt will bring Pops as soon as she gets off shift."

"How did he get the name Pops?"

"Logan named him that when he was first learning to talk and it just kinda stuck. He prefers it to his given name, Flemming." Peter drew the name out, making it sound absurd.

"You've always been surrounded by your family, haven't you?" That question burned. The light-hearted chatter suddenly weighed heavy on Amber.

"Yeah. For better and worse, when we love each other and annoy each other." Peter chuckled. "And we love Christmas around here." He paused. "When was your favorite Christmas, Amber?"

She reflected on Christmases of the past, nibbling a bit on her lip. *My favorite Christmas?* Memories from childhood came flooding back. "I guess it was when I was ten and we'd just found out that Mom was pregnant with Keith. Ryan was just six and fascinated by all the lights and tinsel, and Cassie . . ." Her voice trailed off into silence and her eyes welled up with tears. *Cassie, oh Cassie! How much I miss you!*

Peter gently touched her hand and she jumped in response. *When did he move closer?*

"What happened to Cassie?"

Amber tried clearing her throat. Peter had lost a sister. He could relate to part of her story. *But what would he think of the rest?*

"She . . . we . . ." Amber tried to get the words out but nothing would come. Her heart wanted to burst. She closed her eyes against the tears, but this time they would not be stopped.

"What on earth?" said Faye. She crossed to where Amber sat on the floor, placing a hand on her back. As Faye pulled Amber's hair back from her face, she said, "What is it?"

And Amber could take no more. The gentleness in Peter's eyes, the tenderness in Faye's touch. For the first time in her life, Amber let the sobs come.

⟡⟡⟡⟡⟡⟡⟡⟡⟡⟡⟡⟡⟡

A long time later, Amber sat comfortably on the couch with Faye. At some point during her cry, Frank had joined them and stuffed his handkerchief into her hand. Her eyes were burning as she began her tale.

"Christmas 1992 was just about perfect. My dad's job was going great and the tree was loaded with presents. I remember I got a stereo that year. We lived in California and my sister Cassie had just learned to ride her bike without training wheels. I think her favorite gift that year was the pink streamers for her handlebars. My brother Ryan was six and completely fascinated by all the lights, and Mom had just told us she was pregnant with Keith."

"Since Ry loved the lights so much, Dad decided that for New Year's we would go down to the beach and watch the fireworks. It was special because normally Mom was so strict about bedtimes. Ry wasn't sure whether to be excited or scared. He couldn't wait to see the lights twinkling, but every time one would crackle or boom, he'd turn his face into Dad's neck," said Amber, grinning at the memory.

"I was freezing and just wanted to go home. But not Cassie. She loved every minute. Her eyes were glued to the sky, watching for each tiny burst, giggling and clapping. And on the drive home she was chattering non-stop. It got on my nerves and I got so frustrated that I yelled at her to be quiet." Amber looked down at her hands.

"Mom screamed too, but not at me. I didn't understand at the time what was happening. The next thing I knew, I was being pulled from the car by a fireman and handed off to EMS workers."

Amber paused in her story and took a couple deep breaths. She'd never shared this with anyone, never been able to think about that night without tears coming to her eyes.

"I found out later that a drunk driver had crossed the center line and slammed right into Cassie's door. She never had a chance of surviving. The rest of us escaped with lots of bumps and bruises. Dad had to get stitches in both arms from trying to get to Cassie."

"Oh, dear one," said Faye. "I am so terribly sorry." Faye grabbed Amber's hands and squeezed gently.

"What happened after that, Amber?" said Peter.

Amber looked at him, fresh tears streaming down her cheeks. "Dad didn't know what to do after Cassie died. He started drinking. Mom wasn't doing well with the pregnancy, and after Keith was born, she was pretty sick for a while. Dad started missing work and after a few months, he was fired. We lost the house and had to move in with Mom's parents. After that, Dad got worse. He was always so angry."

Amber got quiet for a moment, lost in her memories.

"So one day you left and never looked back," said Peter.

Amber nodded in agreement. Looking down at Faye's hand covering her own, she continued. "I've worked all kinds of odd jobs, mostly cheap restaurants. Coworkers would normally let me sleep on their couch or sometimes give me a room in exchange for rent when the job paid better. Occasionally a boss would let me sleep in a back room. But I've stayed on the move. I couldn't risk caring about people. I didn't trust them to be the same the next day."

"When my Jamie died, I lost my mind for a while too," said Faye. "I hurt so bad, felt so lonely in my own home surrounded by Frank and my other kids. But the reality was that I was angry at God. At His audacity of taking the precious child He'd given me to watch over. I'm sure I was awful to live with around that time. People in pain frequently are. Unfortunately, knowing why someone hurts doesn't always make the pain they cause us any easier to take. You had to figure out how to deal with your own pain of losing Cassie, as well as everything your daddy was throwing at you."

"I know I'm not much for words," said Frank, "but I'll tell you this. You fit in here with us and you are dear to my heart. As far as I'm concerned, that room upstairs is yours for as long as you're a-wantin' it."

Amber smiled appreciatively at Frank then looked at Peter. He looked steadily into her eyes. "You're safe here, Amber."

"I'm figuring that out." Amber smiled at Peter then looked at Faye.

"Of course you are. Now, I don't know about you, but I'm thinking that what we need tonight is a hearty dinner followed by ice cream and a funny movie. Anyone up for helping in the kitchen?"

"I'd be honored," said Amber. Faye squeezed her tight and looked toward her two men.

"You'll have more left for dinner if I stay out of the kitchen," said Frank.

"True 'nough," said Faye as she and Amber giggled.

"Mom, if you and Amber can handle it, I'm going to head down the path for a bit. Andy said he'd meet me tonight."

"Sounds good. Just come back here for dinner in a couple hours. Now then, Amber, how's chicken and dumplin's sound?"

"Umm . . . what exactly is a dumplin'?"

Chapter 9

"**M**OM SAID I'D FIND YOU out here."

"Hey, Logan! What are you doing here on a Saturday morning?" Peter sat his drill on a shelf and wiped his forehead with his shirt sleeve.

"Dropping off some presents for the kids. Brittney got them some new snow toys that she wanted opened at Mom and Dad's." Logan took in the changes at the house Peter was building for himself. His point of view in the kitchen with about half the cabinets hanging on the wall showed it was starting to look pretty good. "You've done a lot since last time I was out here. I don't think this drywall was up yet."

"Yeah. The master bath is working now and drywall is up and ready to paint everywhere except the back bedroom and the loft."

"Still building this house all by yourself?"

"Mostly. Andy comes out to help three or four times a week."

"Three or four times a week?"

"Yeah. Give or take."

"Come on, Pete. You've not seriously touched this house in weeks. Then a few days back Mom sees you coming out here, disappearing for hours at a time. And not only are you obviously working on it like crazy, you've got Andy coming out to help three or four times a week? What's really going on?"

Peter sighed deeply, running his hand through his hair. "I've got to get out of Mom and Dad's." Peter looked directly at Logan. "I can't live there while Amber is just down the hall."

"Amber? Do you think you and her could turn into something?"

"I don't know. She's beginning to show interest in God, but she's also just beginning to trust again for the first time in sixteen years. I don't know what the future holds. I just know I can't stay there."

Logan looked at Peter for another moment then nodded briefly. "Okay. I've got a couple hours before Heather needs me back at home. What do you want me to do?"

Peter pulled up outside Stephanie's condo and knew she wouldn't be happy. He was running about twenty minutes late. The bellman granted him access to the elevator, and as she opened her door he started with an apology.

"Sorry, Stephanie. I was working on something and lost track of time."

"As long as that something was my Christmas present."

Peter chose to stay quiet. Standing in the entry of her penthouse overlooking Portland, how could he tell her of his log cabin in the woods? She wouldn't understand his choice.

"Speaking of Christmas," she began, "I have a present for you. More than one, actually, but one that you can have now."

He held out her coat, hoping this would spur her out the door and on to dinner.

"Don't you want to know what your present is?" She crossed her slender arms in front of her cherry-colored, cowl-neck dress. The ruched waist with floral beading added a touch of blue, accented by her turquoise earrings. She made a beautiful picture, but Peter was more interested in getting some food in his belly. He'd been so busy at the house that he hadn't eaten anything since a quick sandwich at lunch.

"Well?" said Stephanie.

"Can't you tell me over dinner?"

"No! This is good! I talked to Daddy. He's prepared to offer you a job."

She smiled broadly but Peter didn't quite know how to respond. "What exactly does Malone Industries want with a Forest Engineer?"

"Does it matter? You can finally move to Portland and leave Mayberry behind."

"Stephanie, Forest Engineers tend to like the forest."

"Portland has trees."

"And a lot of cement."

"With the salary Daddy is offering, you could buy a house in Northwest Skyline and have all the trees you want."

"I don't want to live in Northwest Skyline. I like Crossing. I like being ten minutes outside of a town with less than a thousand people."

Stephanie's eyes narrowed, but Peter kept going.

"I like that my parents live there, and my best friend. And I love my dad's logging business."

"Are you actually turning down the job?"

"Please tell your father that I appreciate the offer, but I'm not interested in a job in Portland."

"You're not interested? It's that girl!"

"Girl?"

"I knew she was trouble when I saw you four at lunch yesterday."

"Amber?"

Stephanie pointed her finger at Peter as she continued. "She's trying to get in with your family, get some kind of commitment out of you."

"That's enough." Peter's voice almost growled with the warning.

"She thinks she's found her bank roll, a family so bent on saving the world that they don't see she's cleaning them out!"

"Stephanie! Enough! Your opinion of people has always been harsh but I've overlooked it, hoping you would see a better way."

"Looking at the glass as half-full doesn't get you very far in life. People will take advantage of you."

"If the alternative is to expect the worst of people, to use them before they use me, then I'd rather be taken advantage of," said Peter.

"And what are you going to do?" Stephanie's face contorted, showing her disgust. "Take over Daddy's business? Grow old and die in Crossing?"

"Maybe. I don't have a problem with that. I'm not out to be rich or make some huge mark on the world, Stephanie. I'm always going to choose people over money, relationships over popularity."

He handed her the coat he'd been holding and turned to leave. "I've never fully understood why you kept chasing after me. . . ."

"I do not chase," said Stephanie.

"Maybe, but I think this friendship has reached its end."

"Wait. Peter, perhaps I've been a tad rash. Maybe I've not given Crossing a fair trial."

The corners of Peter's eyes squinted. *Lord, it's hard to believe she's being genuine.*

Stephanie moved closer to him, taking his hand. "You know how upset I get when things don't happen on schedule. I was just thrown off by you being late. That's all. Let's not fight anymore, hmm? Let's go out to dinner."

"I don't think I'm hungry anymore, Steph. Tell you what. You want to give Crossing another chance? Make Mom and Dad's Christmas party in two weeks."

And with that, Peter walked out the door.

<hr />

Peter walked into the darkened kitchen with a heavy sigh. This night was not turning out well. He'd ranted to God for a good fifteen minutes on the drive home then settled down and tried to earnestly pray the rest of the way. He found lots of silence coming out of Heaven tonight.

"Peter. You're home early."

"Hey, Mom."

"Hmm. Quiet, too." Faye walked over to the stove with three mugs. "I suppose things did not go well at dinner tonight?"

Peter yanked his tie off and popped the top button. "We never made it to dinner. Stephanie talked her dad into offering me a job."

"With Malone Industries?"

"Yeah."

"Well, that's quite an opportunity."

Peter ran his hand through his hair. "I don't want to work with Malone Industries, Mom. I want to stay in Crossing."

"I know that, dear." Faye turned to the fridge and began pulling out food. "Let me make you a sandwich."

"Mom, what do you do when you're not sure what God means? I've prayed, I've heard what He's said, but I'm still not sure what He's doing, what He wants."

"Well, you keep doing the last thing you know for sure He told you to do. You persevere and keep praying, asking for guidance and confirmation. Ask for wisdom. He loves to hand out wisdom. And clear vision to see is helpful too. His eyes see so much better than ours."

Faye handed Peter his sandwich. "Why don't you eat that and then grab some hot chocolate from the pot on the stove and join us outside around the fire? Your dad and Amber are having a very interesting conversation. She asked how we know God is trustworthy."

Chapter 10

MATTHEW BRUSHED A BIT OF snow off the legs of his jeans and shifted on the hard bench seat. "The last place I found said she worked there for about four months, which seems to be a record for Portland. She washed dishes. A lady who worked there said they roomed together for a while. One day she just packed up and left. The woman really couldn't tell me much except she talked about going east."

"How long ago was that?" said Thomas.

"Only about a month."

"We were so close!" said Victoria.

Thomas looked Victoria in her dark brown eyes. "We'll find her. It can't be much longer now." He looked back at Matthew. "So, now what?"

He turned his blue eyes out the picture window of the truck stop to watch the snowflakes glide down. "She likes to avoid the main roads. I recommend we head down 26. There's a couple of towns before it junctions with 35 that she may have found a place to stay. Winter's not the time to be roaming around Oregon, and she's a smart girl. She'll hole up somewhere."

Chapter 11

"CAN I ASK YOU A question, Peter?" Amber sat in her usual chair by the fire, the book he had given her to read in her lap.

He finished stacking fresh wood on the hearth and brushed wood chips from his navy blue sweater. "Sure. What's up?"

"After Jamie died, how did you know that God still cared?"

"Wow. Well, I suppose at eight years old it wasn't something I really thought about." Peter placed an arm on the mantelshelf and thought for a moment.

"I guess part of the answer is that I see so much of God's concern for me in other places. I see it in the forest of trees that I love so much, and the sun and rain that He put in place to care for them. I see it in the friends who loved and supported us then, and stuck with Mom even when she tried to push them away. I see His hope in every newborn and His favor all over Dad's logging company."

"But how do you know it's not just luck or karma or positive thinking or hard work? What about all the bad things that happen? What about criminals that get rich or crazy men who take over countries and kill millions of people? What about . . ."

Amber paused for a moment and grew very quiet. "What about when children die?"

"Hmm." Peter sighed. "At some point, every Christian must decide how much he trusts God. You see, if I trust Him, then I have to trust His Word in the Bible, and if I trust His Bible then I have to trust in the part that says God is good, even when I don't like or understand what's going on around me."

"But how can you trust Him when He took someone you love away?"

"He didn't take her, Amber. He allowed her to die. Why?" Peter ran his hand through his hair. "I don't know. It's one of those things that doesn't seem fair. I've missed her over the years, wondering what life would have been like with two sisters, what she would have chosen to do after high school. But even in the midst of the pain, I remind myself that God promised He would never leave us. He gets awfully quiet sometimes, but He's still here."

Amber turned her face toward the fire and thought about Peter's words.

"How old was Cassie?"

Amber sighed deeply. "Eight." Tears started to well up and then slip down her cheeks. She let them flow.

Peter moved to the ottoman in front of her and reached for her hand. "I'm sorry, Amber."

For once she held onto Peter's hand, accepting the comfort he offered. It felt good to finally share part of her burden with someone, but questions continued to roll through her mind. "I was just reading where Kate is struggling to understand the balance between God's justice and mercy. I understand that if Jesus really died on the cross, then, for whatever reason, He accepted the penalty of all we've done wrong. And if we believe that, then God gives us the chance to receive mercy." Amber paused and looked Peter in the eye. "But, what if I don't want someone to receive mercy? I'm not sure what God's justice is supposed to be, but I don't care! It can't be bad enough for this man. Does that make me an awful person? Does that mean I shouldn't have mercy either?"

"Of course not. Amber, this man did something thoughtless and because of it he hurt your family. It's normal to be angry with him. He took something very precious from you. You should be mad! But you can't live there. Anger will destroy you."

Amber yanked her hand out of Peter's and got up to stand at the hearth. "So I'm just supposed to forgive and forget and wait for this God of yours to enact His justice? That man destroyed my family! He took everything!"

"Forgiveness is not forgetting what happened," said Peter. "It's not even giving him a pardon for taking your sister from you. It's simply giving up the right to be angry, trusting God that somehow justice will be achieved." He stood and grabbed Amber by the shoulders, gently turning her around to face him. "Amber, even if you found this man and enacted whatever punishment on him you thought you wanted, you would not receive what you really want. Nothing you do to him will bring your sister back to you or heal your family."

Amber felt her knees going out underneath her. The tears again came in a flood and she cried out as she collapsed into Peter's arms. "Cassie!"

<><><><><><><><><><>

The house was definitely quieter without Peter and Sassy. Amber wandered downstairs and found Faye working on cookies. "Want to help me frost the sugar cookies?"

"Sure." Amber sat down on a stool at the breakfast bar and looked at the variety of icings. "Does it matter which color I use?"

"Nope. Just have fun with it."

Faye hummed as she removed cookies from a tray and replaced them with cookie dough.

"Do you sometimes have trouble remembering Jamie?"

Faye stopped spooning dough for a moment. "Yes. Sometimes in my dreams I can see her so clearly. But in the daytime, it's harder. Sometimes family gatherings are tough because I miss her so much, and sometimes I barely remember she's missing."

"I'm not sure what Cassie looked like anymore."

Faye put down the bowl of cookie dough and walked over to face Amber. She reached for her hand. "Tell me what you do remember."

"Her hair was lighter than mine and always seemed to reflect the sun. And her eyes were more green than brown, and they sparkled."

"Sounds like jealousy colored your vision when you were younger, and now I bet pain does."

"What do you mean?"

"You, my dear, are a beautiful young lady. Your hair is so thick and naturally dark. It's the color of mahogany, something I always wanted instead of this blonde mop God decided for me. Your hair emphasizes your eyes and brings out the darkness of them. It's a natural beauty that women like me work hard to mimic."

Amber couldn't quite believe it. *Could Faye be exaggerating? Me? Beautiful?* She wasn't sure how to respond.

The oven timer dinged and Faye went over to remove cookies from the oven.

"Now then, if you want to remember your sister in a more productive way, why don't you think of some way to honor her?"

Honor her? "I'm not sure how to do that," said Amber.

"Well, what did she like? What would mean something to you? Maybe think of something you could look at that would remind you of how much you love her. For example, when my Jamie died, Frank and I planted that maple out front. It reminds me of her. And when I'm missing her, I can look at it and remember her bouncing down the stairs in the morning or tearing across the yard after her brothers."

Faye and Amber worked in silence for a short time. Faye had given her a lot to think about, and although she didn't have any idea how to honor Cassie, she liked the thought.

She was just finishing up the icing on a cookie when Sassy came bounding through the dog door and pounced on her.

"Sassy!" said Amber.

"Sassy! You get down!" said Faye. "Whatever are you thinking?" She came around the counter to look at Amber. "Are you okay?"

Amber giggled. "Yeah. She just surprised me. What is she doing here?"

"I'm not sure. Maybe she's just not used to staying out at Peter's yet. Still thinks of this as home."

"How long have you had her?" Amber rubbed behind Sassy's ears.

"Oh, since she was a pup. Frank picked her up for Peter as a Christmas present. Let me see, I guess it was five years ago now. He'd just come home from college and was struggling to find his place here and at the logging office. He and his daddy were buttin' heads over the new foresting techniques he'd learned over at Oregon State. She was a bit of a peace offering, I think."

"Mom, did Sass . . ." Peter came in the dining room doors with bright red cheeks and huffing like he'd been running. "Sassy!" Sassy promptly sat at Amber's feet. "Ugh! Dog!"

Amber laughed. She'd never seen Peter this out of sorts before and it was refreshing.

"This is all your fault, you know," Peter said, pointing his finger at Amber.

"Mine?"

"Yes. You know why she comes here."

"I do?" Amber looked from Peter to Faye and back at Peter again.

Peter looked straight at Sassy. "She's a traitor!" Sassy tilted her head at him.

"Really, Peter. Whatever are you talking about?" said Faye.

"She comes here to be with Amber, Mom!"

"Me?" Amber couldn't quite believe it. Sassy had definitely won her heart and Amber knew she could trust Sass, but could the dog really prefer her to Peter?

Sassy barked and jumped up once again, plopping her front paws into Amber's lap.

"Sassy!" all three adults said together.

"What's going on in here?" Frank entered the kitchen with a book in his hand. "You guys are loud enough to wake the dead!"

"My dog has left me for Amber!"

Frank looked at Sassy half lying in Amber's lap. "Well, I always did say she could pick the best treat out of the bag 'fore the rest of us knew the bag was there."

"Dad!"

"But beware, son. Once the women folk gang up on ya, it's all over!"

"Ugh! You're no help. Might as well get her another food bowl for here." Peter muttered something incomprehensible as he stormed out the mudroom door, slamming it behind him.

Amber and Faye looked at each other and started laughing.

Frank stole a cookie and headed back to his chair. "I knew that dog had good brains in her."

As Faye headed to put more cookies into the oven, Amber rubbed Sassy's neck. "Well, girl, I guess it's you and me for a while."

Chapter 12

"**H**ER OPENING UP ABOUT HER sister is good progress." Andy hoisted the drywall into place while Peter screwed it into the wall.

"Yeah. And she's asking some great questions. When I got home from Portland a couple weeks ago, Dad was telling her about our move out here, the step of faith it was for him not knowing if he could get a logging business up and running. She listened carefully, but she admitted that she wasn't quite sure what to think. She was balancing Dad's belief in God's provision with the possibility of dumb luck and hard work."

"I can see your mom jumping all over that one."

Peter chuckled as he put the drill down and opened up the mud bucket. "Yeah. She basically told her that no one could convince her one way or the other. She was just going to have to decide for herself which she thought was the most likely."

"Free will at its best."

"Or worst."

"Pete, do you really think she'll end up walking away?"

"I don't know, Andy. Cassie's dying really caused a lot of turmoil in her family. She's been running from dealing with it for years."

"Maybe she was running. I think God has her right where He's been waiting for her."

"Maybe. We did have an interesting conversation earlier this week about the resurrection. She wanted to know if any evidence outside the Bible existed to prove Jesus came back to life."

"Man! She asks some great questions! If she ever wants to try out law, let me know!" Andy smiled broadly.

"How about less chatter and more mud on that seam!" Peter pointed his drywall knife at the wall beside Andy. *It's not that I think she'll ever leave Mom*, he thought. *But would she stay for more than Mom?*

"Touch-y! What? Don't want her working all the way in Crossing?"

Time to derail this conversation. "I heard Allie talking to Mom about babies at Thanksgiving."

Andy froze just as he was about to apply more mud to the wall. He turned to look at Peter, his eyes narrowing a bit. "How about we get this first coat of mud done so I can get home. I told Allie I'd be home before 10:00 p.m."

"10:00 p.m., huh?" Peter feigned innocence best he could. But a smirk resisted his best effort.

Andy just turned and threw a rag at him. "Get to work!"

◇◇◇◇◇◇◇◇◇◇◇◇◇◇◇◇

"Peter? You here?"

"Hey, Dad! I'm in the kitchen."

"Your mother sent over some chili for lunch."

"Great!"

Peter washed his hands and grabbed a spoon. "Want some?"

"No, thanks. Had some with your mom and Amber before I came here. Place is really looking good." Frank looked over the walnut cabinets and multi-colored Brazilian walnut floor. The large stainless steel refrigerator almost looked out of place in the midst of all the wood.

"Yeah, it's coming along. The countertop is in and should be installed Monday. That just about finishes off the kitchen."

"What did you end up going with?"

"The black engineered stone with blue chunks. You were right. I do like the stones in it, as well as the easy maintenance." Peter grabbed a glass and filled it with water.

"Hmm. Got anyone in mind?"

"To install it?"

"To live here with you. You've been working hard most nights, even got Andy and Logan out here with you. Just wondering if there's a purpose behind it besides you gettin' out of my house."

Peter swallowed his bite of chili and looked at his dad. "Not sure, Dad. Hoping, perhaps. Working towards it, maybe. I just . . . I don't know."

Frank nodded. "Yeah. Well, you keep workin' and let God guide the rest. It'll be fine." He walked over to the sink and looked out the window. The trees encircling the small back-yard looked like a snow-covered paradise in the daylight.

Peter looked at his father for a moment. *God, what is going on here?* "Dad what's really going through your mind? You're almost speaking in riddles and only half making sense."

"Pete, I know we've had our differences over the years. Your mom and I knew one day you'd move out, and six months ago we worried about your lack of work on this house. We didn't want you to focus so much on takin' care of us that you lost track of what you wanted."

Frank turned to face Peter. "The past couple of weeks we've been praying a lot. The path of marriage is a great one, full of amazin' joys and sometimes tremendous heartache. But it only works with a person who wants to dedicate herself to walkin' with you."

"I know, Dad. I'm walking carefully, praying constantly."

"I don't s'pose we can ask any more. Whatever you decide, know I'm proud of you, son. God's honored your mother's prayers that you'd be strong and compassionate and absolutely in love with Jesus."

"Thanks, Dad. That means a lot."

"Well, I'd best be gettin' back. Don't you be late tonight. Your mother's cookin' up a storm for her Christmas party."

"I'll be along in a bit."

Frank walked to the front door and looked around once more. "Yep. Needs a woman's touch in here." He was out the door and in his truck before Peter could reply.

He shook his head as he looked around himself. The party started in about four hours, so he thought he would have time to finish hooking up the dishwasher and get the new lights in the extra bedrooms working. *He's right, Daddy. I'm praying You and I have the same girl in mind, but if not, please make it clear before my heart gets lost in her any more than it already has.*

Ready to go to the party, Peter walked into the kitchen and put his glass into the dishwasher. "Well, I guess I will try you out tomorrow after breakfast to make sure you work without leaking. I can't quite start you with nothing more than a bowl and a spoon from lunch and my water glass."

He looked around, taking in the new light blue paint on the walls. "God, I know You've got things in hand, but this dishwasher just looks so empty. And the house is quiet with only me here. I'm used to having people around." *Or at least Sassy*, he thought.

Faith, Peter.

"Yes, Lord. I see Your hand moving. I do."

Hope, Peter.

"My hope grows stronger each week. But is the one I'm hoping for the one You have planned for me? That pesky free will thing keeps coming up."

Love her.

Peter sighed deeply and looked out the window at the same trees his dad had looked at earlier. They sparkled in the moonlight, rivaling any indoor Christmas tree he'd ever seen.

"I do, Lord. Please draw her."

Peter walked over to the back door and turned off the lights. He stopped to look again at the back yard when he saw something in the trees. He looked closer and felt sure he saw the face of a man. "What the—?" He opened the door and yelled, "Can I help you?"

The man locked his eyes onto Peter. Peter felt strange, like he was being drawn toward the man. He was almost eager to go to him, not apprehensive. The man stood quietly at the edge of the trees in his coat and blue jeans, seemingly not cold in the dropping temperatures.

"Sir?"

The man dipped his head slightly at Peter then turned to walk away. Peter jumped off the deck and began to run in his direction. "Wait!"

Peter was at the trees in just seconds, but he couldn't see the man anywhere. He looked at the place where he'd last seen him.

No footprints!

Suddenly, Peter noticed how cold the night was becoming.

Chapter 13

THE WINTER NIGHT AIR FELT good against Amber's flushed cheeks. The annual Christmas party had turned a normally spacious house into a gathering place for wall-to-wall people. The Christmas tree was beautiful, and while Christmas decorations of every kind covered the banister, mantel, bookshelves, and doorways, food covered all the available tables and counters: ham, turkey, meatballs, cheeses, breads, fruits, cookies, and cupcakes. Faye had prepared all week for this feast and it looked like the whole town had showed up.

Amber looked down at Sassy. "Too many people for my taste, girl."

The dog wagged her tail in response.

Amber turned to look through the French doors at the interesting mix of people inside. *It looks like Micah and Frank are following orders again.* Faye had kept them busy adding chairs for people to sit in, taking coats, and slicing meat. Amber was in charge of the punch bowl, keeping it full and cold, while Peter had been assigned trash and parking duty.

Suddenly the door opened and Peter walked out with Amy. "Okay. You sit here for a minute and I'll grab your coat." Amber watched Peter go back inside. He left the young brunette sitting in one of the chairs around the fire bowl just outside the French doors. Amber felt the need to be polite but wasn't sure what to say.

"Hi."

"Hey, Amber. It's nice to fin'ly meet you. We didn't really get a chance to say much at Thanksgivin'."

Peter came back through the door. "Here, Amy. Cover up with this blanket. Amber, will you watch over her while I go find Chad?" Without pausing for an answer, he turned back into the throb of people. Amber felt a bit uneasy with her new charge. *Now what do I say?*

"You really don't have to stay out 'ere wit' me if you're wantin' to go back in. I just got overheated, that's all. A couple minutes out 'ere 'n I'm sure I'll be fine."

Amber thought back to the soup Faye had fixed for Amy. *That seems like so long ago.* "Are you feeling better? I know you were sick for a while."

"Oh, some. It comes and goes. Thankfully now the mornin' sickness is mostly gone, but I get so hot. I was 'bout to die in there wit' all those folks!"

"Can I get you a drink?" Amber nervously watched the door, starting to shiver some herself. *Peter, where are you? Should Amy be out here in the cold like this?*

"No, thanks. 'Twas my own fault really. I shoulda never sat down by the fire."

Now what do I say? Why does my mind always go blank when I'm face to face with people?

Thankfully Amy breached the quiet. "How you likin' Crossin'?"

"It's a nice town. Although I think I like it better out here."

"Yeah, us too."

"Where do you live?"

"Oh, we just have a small place down from the loggin' office a bit. We didn't have much when we got married. Chad has worked for Frank ever since he was a kid, runnin' errands and whatever else Frank could think of to keep him busy. He knew Chad's always wanted a place of his own out 'ere, so as a wedding present he gave us a small piece of land."

Wow. "That was nice."

"Little Joshua can't wait 'til he turns seven. Frank's promised him he can start workin' some just like his daddy did."

"Amy!" Chad burst through the door with Peter close behind, immediately crouching beside his wife's chair. "Are you a'right? Let me take you on home. We'll—"

"No, not yet. Please, Chad. I'm fine. Really. I just got overheated. The kids are likin' the time out and I'm enjoyin' the break from havin' to watch Caleb so close."

Amber felt like she was intruding on a private moment, but with Chad's lowered stance in front of the door, she couldn't easily sneak away.

"You've been out in this cold long enough. How 'bout I get you a seat in the kitchen near Faye. I'll feel better stayin' if I know she's watchin' over you."

"Okay. That'd be nice. It was nice to talk wit' you, Amber."

"You too, Amy."

As Chad walked her inside, Peter crossed over to Amber and handed her his wool-lined denim jacket. "We can't have you catching a cold five days before Christmas."

"Thank you."

"Thanks for watching over her for me. She wasn't looking too good inside."

"She seems really sweet."

"She is. They are a neat couple who've overcome a lot."

"Like what?"

"Amy's parents died when she was young and she was raised by her grandmother, who died shortly after they got married. Chad's dad . . . well. . . . Let's just say he was more concerned about his next drink than he was about his family eating. Chad's mom couldn't take it anymore and took off when Chad was about six or seven years old. So Dad kinda took him under his wing and made sure he stayed out of trouble. Went toe-to-toe with the man a couple of times about school supplies and new shoes. Stuff like that. Dad always had some hope that he would get things turned around."

"Is he still around here?"

"No. He took off one night when Chad was about sixteen. An aunt took Chad in until he graduated and could start working with Dad full time."

This family. They continued to amaze her. Who took that much care about a boy with both a father and an aunt? Who gave away land as a wedding present?

Isn't it nice to be part of a family, Amber?

Yes. Wait. She looked at Peter. *Did he say that? I don't think so. Where did that come from?*

"Are you ready to go back inside?"

"I'm not sure. It's a little overwhelming," said Amber.

Peter's eyes softened as he held her gaze. "Don't worry about it. There's a lot of people in there. It's overwhelming for me and I know all of them."

Amber hesitated. Peter stood so close. *If only I had the right to reach out to him, walk back into the house on his arm. Would he want me to?* She looked into his eyes, silently asking for reassurance.

"Am I interrupting something?"

Amber cringed at the syrupy sweetness in Stephanie's voice. *Can Peter really not know what she's like?*

"Stephanie! I'm glad you could make it down here tonight. You remember Amber?"

"Of course." Stephanie glided over toward Peter and looped her arm through his before turning her cool stare toward Amber. "Isn't it nice, Amber, that you are able to participate in Faye's little party this year."

Amber wasn't sure if she felt the insult more for herself or for Faye. More fitting for a night in the city rather than the simple town gathering inside, Stephanie's cashmere sweater sparkled in the moonlight. *The princess certainly knows how to play up her strengths.*

"Isn't it." Amber couldn't help the icy tone in her own voice.

"How thoughtful of you, sweetheart, to loan Amber your coat so she wouldn't be cold. Really, Amber, you need to replace that *thing* you were wearing last time I saw you."

Her eyes obviously didn't miss much.

"Would you be a dear, Amber, and go fetch me a drink. I'm simply parched from the long drive here."

Summarily dismissed, Amber strode angrily toward the door. *Peter may think she's good company, but I don't have to put up with her! And she can get her own drink!*

Amber watched the family drive away Sunday morning in Peter's Jeep, Faye's words from a couple weeks ago echoing in her mind: "You'll have to decide for yourself."

Amber sighed deeply, nibbling on her bottom lip. *So, God, how does this work? Let's just say I'm curious.*

Silence.

"Well, what did you expect? Great. Now I'm talking to myself."

Sassy whimpered at her feet.

"Maybe I'll just pretend I was talking to you, girl."

Amber eyed the library with its shelf of Bibles. "Well, I guess if the lady in the book started with the Gospel of Luke, that's where I'll start too." Amber flipped through the pages as she walked to her chair by the fire.

Amber found Luke and began to read.

Many have undertaken to draw up an account of the things that have been fulfilled among us, just as they were handed down to us by those who from the first were eyewitnesses and servants of the word. With this in mind, since I myself have carefully investigated everything from the beginning, I too decided to write an orderly account for you. . . .

Chapter 14

THE HOUSE WAS FULL OF activity when Peter walked through his parents' door on Christmas Eve. Sassy bounded toward him and he reached down to give her a quick rub around the ears.

"Hey, Mom!" As he walked to the tree with the last of his presents, he couldn't help but look around for Amber, finally noticing her and Brittney sitting at the breakfast bar together.

"Uncle Peter!" Emma came racing across the living room with her arms stretched wide. He scooped her up and swung her around in a big circle before wrapping her tight in a bear hug. She giggled in delight.

Right behind her was two-year-old Taylor. "Unc Pe-er! Me too!"

Laughing, Peter set Emma down. "You bet, munchkin! Come here!"

"Uncle Peter, will you play Candyland with me?" said Emma.

"Me too!" said Taylor.

"Gotta watch that little one, Peter. She cheats!"

Peter grinned at Pops sitting at the chess table across from his dad. "Sounds like she's been taking lessons from her great grandfather!"

"She's a smart girl!" said Pops.

"Pops, really!" said Heather. "Hey, Pete!" Heather walked over to give him a hug.

"Uncle Peter! Candyland?" said Emma.

Logan walked into the room carrying six-month-old Megan. "Mom! Pete's here. Can we eat now?"

"I told you that you should have eaten lunch," said Heather.

"I wasn't hungry then. Mom!"

"Logan William. Would you kindly stop yelling at me from the other room," said Faye.

"I'm hungry!" said Logan.

"And whiny!" said Faye, laughing. "Come on, everyone. Let's gather for prayer before Logan regresses any farther!"

◇◇◇◇◇◇◇◇◇◇◇◇◇◇◇

Dinner was a noisy affair and Peter noticed that everyone was in a great mood. Even Amber. *Father, she's interacting with the family like . . . well, like she belongs.*

At that moment Amber was giggling with Brittney over some story from their childhood. "What are you two talking about?" said Peter.

"Britt's telling her about the time when she tricked you into doing the dishes after she rigged the sprayer to douse you when you turned the water on," said Logan.

"I remember that one," said Faye, giggling at the memory. "I was working on some laundry and next thing I knew, you were yelling at your sister. You must have turned the water on full blast because you were soaked!"

Everyone at the table laughed.

Peter rolled his eyes. "I had turned the water on all the way. And as I remember, I was so mad because we were getting ready to leave. I had to go change clothes and then Dad was irritated at having to wait for me."

Frank chuckled. "It was a good prank."

"Now I know you didn't leave it at that," said Heather. "What'd you do to get her back?"

"He locked me in my room!" said Brittney.

"Now how'd he do that?" said Faye. "I don't remember that."

"That's because he waited until you and Dad were out for a walk," said Brittney.

Logan and Peter burst out laughing.

"How'd you lock her in?" said Pops. "Doesn't her door lock from the inside?"

"Yeah," said Peter. "We turned the door knob around."

"We had to wait for several days," said Logan, "before we had the time to get the knob turned around, Britt in her room, and you guys out of the house."

Amber looked at Brittney. "What did you do?"

"I climbed out the window and about broke my neck!"

Peter shook his head as he grinned. Life at the Yager house had certainly never been dull!

"Is that how that lattice got broke?" said Frank.

"Yeah," said Brittney. "I made it out the window and to the lattice okay, but partway down, one of the boards broke and I fell the rest of the way. I was sore for three days!"

"And we felt bad for two!" said Logan as he and Peter exchanged looks and burst out laughing all over again.

"Sometimes I wonder that any of you survived childhood," said Faye.

◇◇◇◇×◇◇×◇◇×◇◇×◇◇

Presents had been opened and lots of games of Candyland played with Emma and Taylor before Logan and Heather packed them up to go home. Brittney and Pops had left shortly after that. Now Frank, Faye, Peter, and Amber sat relaxing in the living room with cups of hot chocolate.

Peter looked at the clock. "Are you going to the Christmas Eve service tonight?"

"Of course, dear," said Faye. "What time is it?"

"Almost 8:30, Mom."

"My goodness. I'd better get ready. Amber, are you ready?" Faye shuffled off without waiting for an answer.

Peter gave his mom a surprised look, then looked at Amber.

"Come on, Frank. You need a clean shirt," said Faye.

Frank got up to follow his wife down the hall. "I expect dear-heart has somethin' to tell you, Peter."

Peter looked at Amber, trying not to hold his breath. She looked at him, then down at her hands. Nibbling a little on her lower lip, she took a deep breath.

"When you all left for church on Sunday, I was curious. So I looked up the book of Luke and started reading. It was interesting, until I got to this one story where Jesus healed a lady. He was on His way with some important synagogue leader to heal the man's daughter, when a lady in the crowd touched His clothes."

Amber paused and Peter wasn't sure whether to say something or remain quiet. *Speaking might be more encouraging.* "I know the story. She'd been to many different doctors and no one could help her."

"Well, it really hit me that Jesus stopped what He was doing with this important man to help some poor lady, a stranger. He could have pretended that He didn't notice; after all, no one else did. He could have shouted out 'You're welcome!' and kept going. But He didn't do that either. He stopped to talk to her, to acknowledge her, to show her she was just as important as this leader beside Him."

Amber suddenly got up and walked over to the fireplace. Peter guessed she was nervous. He knew how scary it could be sharing your heart with someone. She was taking a huge risk and although he wanted to reassure her, he needed to hear everything she was going to say.

"I realized that Jesus reached out to me too. He stopped whatever else He was doing the day I arrived in Crossing and He somehow put me and your dad together." She turned to face him.

"I've been struggling to understand why your family would take me in when you knew nothing about me. I couldn't figure out why anyone would cook a meal for a sick woman, or care that an old man sat in his home after his wife died. Every time I turned around, one of you was doing something nice for someone else. And your family! The way you just envelop friends, treating Heather and Allie and all the others like they belong here." She paused and looked down at her hands for a moment. "It was just how Jesus treated that woman. It was Him treating me that way too, through all of you."

Hope grew stronger inside Peter. He watched Amber nibble on her lower lip again.

"I decided I didn't want to walk away from that. With my past, if God thinks I'm important enough to meet me here in Oregon, the least I can do is trust Him."

"Trust Him?" Peter barely contained the excitement building in his chest. *Could she possibly mean what I hope she means?*

Amber laced her fingers together. "Monday night I talked to your mom about all this. I told God that I knew He sent Jesus to save me through His death on the cross. I believe God raised Jesus from the dead and now He is with God in Heaven. I asked Him to come heal my heart and show me what to do next."

Peter jumped out of his chair and crossed the space to where Amber was standing. He grabbed her hands and held them tight.

Amber looked back at him, her eyes filling with tears. "You're happy?"

"I don't know if I could adequately tell you how much," said Peter.

As they stood there, Peter clearly heard: *Remember, Peter. Faith, hope, love. But the greatest of these is. . . .*

Yes, Father. Love.

"Come on, you two," said Frank. "Let's not be late tonight!"

Peter gently wiped a tear from Amber's cheek then turned slightly and offered her his arm. "May I escort you to your first Christmas Eve service in Crossing?"

She gently placed her hand on his arm. "I'd be honored."

Chapter 15

MATTHEW STOMPED HIS BOOTS AND opened the door to the Law Office. "Mr. Williams?"

Andy turned from the bookshelf in the conference room and looked at the stranger. "Yes, sir?"

"I'm looking for someone. The sheriff said that you might be helpful."

Andy looked at the man curiously, taking in his blue jeans, hiking boots, and winter coat. "Now why might the sheriff send you to me?"

"He said that since you're the only lawyer in town, everyone comes to you. He also said you often make trips to the outlaying homes and might notice someone new that's avoiding town."

"Well, I suppose that's a good working theory." Andy closed the law book he was holding and walked toward the man. "Who exactly are you looking for?"

"Her name's Rachel. She's in her mid-twenties, about five-foot-two with dark hair and eyes."

"That's not much to go on. . . . I'm sorry. Your name is . . . ?"

"Matthew. Here's a picture, but it's about ten years old."

Andy took the picture and tried not to react. "Is she wanted for some crime?"

"No, nothing like that. Have you seen her about?"

"I can't say for sure. Do you have a number I can reach you at if I have any information to pass on to you?"

"Sure. Here's my card. Call me anytime."

Chapter 16

AMBER FELT LIKE SHE WAS living a dream. As the church sang "Away in a Manger" by candlelight during the Christmas Eve service, tears overflowed once more. *Jesus, You came for me. I don't understand, but thank You.*

As she stood there trying to quietly wipe the tears away, Frank passed her his handkerchief and Peter looked at her with concern. All she could do was smile at him.

Several of those at the service were people she'd met while working at the office. Andy and Allie were there, as well as Micah, who seemed to have found some peace with the season. Everyone was friendly, but considering the hour, few wanted to hang around long after the service.

The drive home was peaceful and Peter dropped them off at the door. Before pulling away he looked at Amber and quietly said, "I'll see you in the morning."

Amber couldn't remember a better Christmas. Faye spoiled her with more new clothes than she could remember owning in many years. And Peter gave her a new winter coat complete with hat, gloves, and a scarf. For the family, Amber had sketched different things: Faye at the logging office for Frank, Sassy lying in front of the couch for Peter, and the maple tree with the face of a child looking down from the sky for Faye.

"Oh, Amber." Tears came to Faye's eyes and Amber went to sit beside her on the couch. "However did you know how to draw Jamie?"

"I just looked at the similarities in your other three," said Amber. "And I asked Peter some questions."

"So that's why you wanted to know if she looked more like Brittney or Logan," said Peter.

"Yeah. All three of you look a lot alike, but you and Brittney are much closer. The shape of Logan's face and jawline is more square and his mouth is more like his father's."

"You're very good," said Faye.

"You ever take any classes?" said Frank.

"Not really," said Amber. "Just what I could pick up here and there. Once in high school I had an art teacher that encouraged me. She gave me a book on some techniques, but it got left behind quite a while ago."

"Hmm. Might should fix that," said Frank.

"I'm impressed, Amber," said Peter. "If this is what you can do with copy paper and a regular pencil, I'd love to know what you'd turn out with more professional grade equipment."

"This is beautiful, my dear," said Faye. "I will treasure it. I think one of our boys here needs to hit the wood shop and make us some frames!"

◇◇◇◇◇◇◇◇◇◇◇◇◇◇◇

Amber stretched and looked at the clock. *7:32. I'd best get moving.* She leaned over the side of the bed and ruffled the fur on Sassy's side. "Come on, girl. It's four days after Christmas and the first day of the work week. I can't lay around all morning!"

She went downstairs to find Faye making pancakes for breakfast. "Morning!"

"Good morning," said Faye. "Sounds like we have a pretty lazy week ahead of us."

"We do?"

"Good morning, my ladies," said Frank. He walked over and grabbed a coffee mug.

"I was just startin' to tell Amber about our week," said Faye.

"If you two can finalize all the paperwork for the Christmas trees this week, I'd much appreciate it. Peter's closin' up things in town, and the men will be workin' on recyclin' whatever is left over. I gotta start thinkin' about makin' sure all the year end paperwork gets together for Allie."

"Do you need any help with that?" said Amber.

"Here," said Faye. "You two start in on these while you talk."

Frank grabbed the platter of pancakes from her and walked over to the table. Amber got the syrup out of the pantry and grabbed orange juice from the refrigerator.

"I was actually wonderin', dear-heart, if maybe you'd like to help take over some of the bills and all down there." He stopped to look at Amber. "I can pay the bills and balance the checkbook, but outside of that I get lost pretty fast." Frank grabbed the syrup and began pouring it over his pancakes. "Oops. Sorry, love."

"Franklin," said Faye. "I wash more tablecloths because of you."

"True 'nough," said Frank. He winked at her, and Faye just shook her head as she giggled back at him.

"Anyway," said Frank, "if you're interested, Faye could arrange some time for you and Allie to sit down and she could train you on a lot of the other stuff she'd like for me to be doin'."

"I think I would like that," said Amber.

"Good. Love, you think you can make time to call Allie and see what she's got time for this next week or two?"

"I'll take care of it."

◇×◇×◇×◇×◇×◇×◇×◇×◇×◇

Peter opened the door slightly and kicked snow off his boots before entering the office Monday afternoon. As he closed the door he looked toward Amber. She was smiling at him. *Man, she's got a great smile. What a difference from just a few weeks ago.*

"Okay, Mom. Here's the final numbers from the tree lot. Chad and Jack are working through the few trees that were left and I hired a couple of the boys hanging out in the square to help finish cleanup."

"Wonderful, Peter." Faye took the papers from him. "Andy called and said he needs to talk to you."

"That's odd. I was in town all morning."

"I got the feeling he was up in Portland," said Faye.

"Hmm. I don't remember him saying he was heading up there for anything. I wonder what's up."

"He wouldn't really say. I could tell he was being careful with his words."

"Did he want me to call him?" said Peter.

"I don't think so," said Faye. "He said he'd look for you at your house later tonight."

"Sounds good. Anything else?"

"No, it's been pretty quiet 'round here. I was thinking about closing up the office early." Faye stacked the papers she was working on neatly and put them to the side of her desk. "Amber, why don't you and Peter go for a walk?"

Sassy barked in response and began wagging her tail.

"The sun is shining beautifully," said Faye, "and it doesn't seem to be too cold out there this afternoon."

"It's actually nice right now," said Peter.

"Are you sure you don't need help with those numbers?" said Amber.

"Nah. We've already done most of what needed done for the week. You two go on and enjoy yourselves."

Peter grabbed Amber's new coat off the rack and held it out for her. He opened the door, and they took off for the spot where just a couple days before he had placed Faye's new bench.

"Your dad's going to get Allie to teach me more of the finances in the office so I can help him with all that."

"Does that mean you're going to be hanging around for a while?"

"I hadn't really thought about it. In fact, I kinda forgot about my plans to move on. That's weird."

"Why?"

"Well, normally after just a couple of weeks I'd be looking for a map so I could figure out where I was and where I needed to go next. But, now . . ." Amber paused. *Life is so different now. Could I really just stay here?*

"Now, what?"

Peter stopped walking and Amber stopped with him. She turned to look at him.

"I think I'd like to stay." Amber began to think about what all that could mean. Flashes of a home of her own, friends, and family passed through her mind. *Two months ago I wouldn't have thought it, but the idea of family and friends sounds comforting.*

Peter smiled and reached for her hand. They started walking again.

After a few minutes, Amber said, "I suppose I should start looking for a place to stay. I can't live with your mom and dad forever."

"I don't think there's a rush. Mom likes you being close."

"Yes, but the original deal was just for three or four months. If I'm thinking about staying here permanently, then I should get a place of my own."

They'd reached the river and Peter brushed the bit of snow off the bench seat so they could sit.

"What about sharing?"

"Sharing? Like a roommate? I don't know about that. It's never worked out great before."

"What about sharing with a husband?"

Amber stopped breathing momentarily. She could barely speak and wasn't sure whether it was safer to look at Peter or the river. She couldn't resist the urge to see what his eyes would tell her. "A husband?"

Peter reached for her hand again. "Look, Amber. I'm certainly not going to rush you down the aisle. I know a lot's been happening inside you over the past month or so. But I do know that I am falling deeply in love with you. I'd like for marriage to be an option at some point in our future."

Amber wasn't sure what to say. *Marriage. Me and Peter?* She stood and walked a few steps closer to the river. "What about Stephanie?"

"Stephanie's not an option for me. Never has been."

"But you saw her so often." Amber's emotions were bubbling to the surface.

"I guess you could say that Stephanie was something to occupy my time. As far as I was concerned, she was never anything more than a friend."

Amber felt like a huge load had been removed. Tears sprung to her eyes and began flowing down her cheeks.

"Anyway, she'd never settle down in Crossing," said Peter, "or like my dad's logging business. She was always pushing, trying to get me to move to Portland, become some executive in her father's business. She just liked the idea of me. I'm not sure she ever liked the man I actually want to become."

Amber couldn't say a word without revealing she was crying. She just stood looking at the river, seeing instead the possibility of life with Peter. *When did that become my dream? The first time we walked down this path together? Over dinner each night?*

"Amber, what do you think?"

She turned and looked at him, tears still streaming down her face. "I don't know what to think! I'm overwhelmed."

Peter came to stand in front of her, taking her hands in his. "What is it, my precious one?"

Amber smiled at him. "First your dad wanted me. Then your mom and your dog." Amber giggled for a moment. "Then I found out Jesus wanted me, and now you do. I feel like the verse you put on your mom's bench. I feel like a 'treasured possession.'"

Chapter 17

"**A**NDY!"

"Hey, Pete. We've got to talk."

"Come on in."

Peter was concerned. He knew his friend valued his home time, and to be away from Allie at almost 9:00 p.m. told him this was important. As Andy walked in, Peter noticed his crumpled suit pants and loosened tie. "You look beat. What's going on?"

Andy sat on the leather couch while Peter took the chair next to him.

"I'm exhausted. I've been working on a new case, of sorts."

"Can you tell me who the client is?"

"I guess you, Pete."

"Me?"

Andy sighed. "A man came into my office the day after Christmas. A stranger to town, looking for a girl."

"A girl? You mean Amber."

"Well, I wasn't sure, so I put him off. The girl he's looking for is named Rachel."

"So, it's not Amber."

"The picture he showed me of her at about fifteen or sixteen is a dead ringer. But I had to be sure, so I did some digging."

Peter didn't know what to think. *My best friend is looking out for me. But he's also digging up information on the woman I love behind my back. Amber's already told me so much. Could there be more?*

"The agency this man works for seems to be legit. They specialize in finding people. Based in Portland, they have a couple offices in California, one in Nevada, and another in Washington State." Andy paused and rubbed his eyes.

"So someone is definitely looking for her but thinks her name is Rachel?"

"I believe so. It turns out her name is Rachel. Amber is her middle name and apparently what she's been going by for a while. Not that the man I talked to last week seemed to know that."

"What else did you find out?"

"Well, she was tough to follow. Everything you've told me about her has checked out. She's moved around a lot the last few years, never staying anywhere that I could find longer than four months. Worked about every low income job there is to be found, but all legitimate businesses. Been in the hospital a couple times. Once was after a dog attack and once included some pretty good contusions she wouldn't explain."

Peter sat forward. *The dog attack explains her fear of Sassy when she first got here, but the contusions . . ? Stuff like that only comes from accidents or beatings. And if she wouldn't tell the doctors anything . . .* "What kind of contusions?"

"On her upper arms like someone had grabbed her and another on the cheek. One of the staff told me her ribs were bruised up pretty good. The doctor wasn't happy when they found out she'd snuck out of the hospital, but shortly after she went missing a brute of a man showed up looking for her."

"What do you know about this man looking for her now, Andy?"

"His name is Matthew." Andy sat forward and put his elbows on his knees. "When he came into the office, he was dressed like he'd been traveling, possibly out looking. Blue jeans, hiking boots, thick winter coat."

Peter felt goosebumps going up his arms. "Blonde hair and bright blue eyes?"

"You've seen him around?"

"I saw him in my backyard!"

Andy looked at Peter, suddenly alert. "When?"

"The night of Mom's party, that Saturday before Christmas." Peter couldn't sit any longer. He paced to the fireplace and back to the couch. "He was standing at the tree line. I was getting ready to head over to Mom and Dad's, so I turned off the lights in the kitchen. That's when I saw him standing there."

"What time was that?

"About 6:00, I guess."

"How did you see him so clearly in the dark?"

Peter tried to remember exactly what had happened. "I don't know. It was like he was standing in daylight, as close to me as you are. But I'm also certain that he was at the tree line at the back of the yard." He ran his hand through his hair. "This doesn't make any sense."

"What else do you remember?"

"I called out to him but he didn't answer. After a moment he just nodded his head at me and turned to leave. I ran out to him, but he was gone."

"Why did he choose your backyard?"

Peter silently walked back to the fireplace while Andy continued. "Does he know where Amber is? If he's connected her to you, then why waste time coming to see me?"

"There's more." Peter knew his friend would believe him, but he struggled to believe it himself. He turned to look at Andy. "When I got out to the tree line, there were no footprints."

"What do you mean no footprints?"

"I mean the snow was not disturbed. It looked like no one had been standing there. No one had walked there or turned to walk away. The only footprints I could find in that entire area were mine coming from the house."

Andy looked at Peter. "You're sure you saw him."

"I wasn't until tonight. But how else would I know about his blonde hair and blue eyes?"

"We've got to talk to Amber, Pete. We've got to know more about what we're dealing with here."

Peter looked at the clock. It was only 9:20 and he knew his parents would be up until at least 10:00. "Let's go now. I won't be able to sleep until I know she's safe."

⬦⬦⬦⬦⬦⬦⬦⬦⬦⬦⬦⬦⬦⬦

"Mom? Dad?" Peter burst through the dining room door with Andy close behind.

"Peter! What on earth . . . ?" said Faye, turning from her spot on the couch to watch her son cross over to them.

"Where's Amber?" said Peter.

"I'm right here." Amber sat in her usual spot by the fire. Relief washed over him.

"Andy!" said Faye.

"What's going on, son?" said Frank.

"We're not sure, Dad, but we all need to talk," said Peter.

"This sounds serious," said Faye.

"We're not sure what it is," said Andy.

Peter took a seat near Amber on the ottoman while Andy sat on the couch beside Faye.

"I should probably start," said Andy, "by telling you that I've spent the day investigating you, Amber."

"Me? Why?"

"A man came to see me Friday."

"What did he want, Andy?" said Frank.

"He showed me a picture of a girl he's trying to find."

"He's looking for Amber?" said Faye.

"Has to be," said Andy as he looked at Amber, "unless you've got a twin out there."

Amber shook her head. "No, no twin."

Peter watched Amber's face get very white. He grabbed her hand and looked into her eyes. "You're safe here, Amber."

She just nodded in response.

"Who is he?" said Amber.

"His name is Matthew. He gave me a card, and everything I could find about the agency he works for checks out. They specialize in finding people."

"Is there anyone," said Peter, "who might hire someone to track you down, Amber? Anyone who might want to hurt you?"

"Peter! Why would you ask that?" said Faye.

"This man was at my house, Mom. The Saturday night of your Christmas party, I saw him out in my yard."

"Doing what, son?" said Frank.

"Dad, I'm not quite sure. When I saw him, he was standing in the tree line. When I spoke to him, he nodded like . . ." Peter ran his hand through his hair. "I don't know. Like we had just agreed to something. He turned to leave, so I ran out to him. But . . ." Peter sighed. "But, he just disappeared."

"You lost him in the woods?" said Faye.

"No, Mom. He was gone, footprints and all. There was no sign of him ever being there."

Amber stood and walked a couple steps away from Peter. Her back to him, he couldn't tell what she was feeling. *Does she believe me? Lord, help us!*

"If it helps any, Amber, the man called you Rachel," said Andy.

"Rachel? Who's Rachel?" said Faye.

Peter watched Amber turn to look at Andy, then down at the carpet as she sat carefully on the edge of the hearth.

Frank broke the silence. "What is it, dear-heart?"

Peter finally saw the tears she was hiding. He went over and crouched before her. He brushed one side of her hair back and put his fingers under her chin, gently lifting until she could look into his eyes. "What's going on? Who is Matthew?"

She grabbed his hand and Peter held firm.

"I don't know this Matthew, but. . . ." She looked at Faye. "I am Rachel."

"It's your first name," said Andy, "and Amber is your middle name."

She nodded. "Yes. I've always hated the name because of my initials. My full name's Rachel Amber Griffin. R-A-G. After Cassie died, I felt like a ragdoll that had been tossed aside and forgotten. When I left home, I refused to be called Rachel. Only my bosses knew my full name. Everyone I worked with just knew me as Amber."

"So whoever is looking for you is from your childhood?" said Peter.

"It has to be family," said Amber. "I haven't been close to anyone in fifteen years. No one from that far back would be looking."

"But that doesn't explain the missing footprints," said Andy.

"Maybe it does," said Faye.

"What do you mean, Mom?" said Peter.

"Look, the more important thing," said Faye, "is what we're going to do now. Amber, do you want to meet this family who's looking for you?"

Andy sat up straighter on the couch. "My guess is that they've worked pretty hard to find you. Your trail is not easy to follow! I suspect that whether you want to meet them or not, they're going to find a way."

"What do you suggest, Andy?" said Frank.

"Matthew left his contact information with me. I suggest that you allow me to call him and say that I know where you are and you're willing to talk with him, under certain conditions. Number one will be telling us whom he's working for. If they are the ones who want to talk, then we meet at my office in Crossing where we can best protect Amber."

Peter looked at Amber and the living room faded away. "What do you think?"

"I don't know if I can do this, Peter."

"I believe you can."

"You want me to do this, don't you?"

"Precious, I believe God made you for more than running from your past."

Amber sighed deeply and looked down. Peter prayed fervently for her to have the courage to do this, no matter what family member was behind Matthew.

"All right." Amber looked back up at Peter, then Andy. "Make the call."

Chapter 18

A MBER TURNED OVER AGAIN. *God, this whole faith thing is new to me. Did you have to start big? Who could be looking for me that knows me as Rachel? Ryan, maybe. He'd be what, twenty-two now? But would he have the resources to hire a detective? Keith would be too young and I don't see Dad caring. Would Mom look for me if something happened to Dad?*

She turned over and looked at the clock. *11:47. I'm not getting any sleep this way.* She sat up and looked at Sassy. "Come on, girl. Let's get some milk."

Amber grabbed her new plush bathrobe, a Christmas present from Brittney, and walked downstairs. A light was on in the library so she walked over to see who else was still up. Faye sat quietly in her rocker looking out the window, her hand resting on the Bible in her lap.

"Trouble sleeping too?" said Amber quietly.

Faye looked at her and smiled. "Yes."

"I was going to get some milk. Can I get you anything?"

"How about something warm? I was just thinking some hot chocolate sounded good."

"That would be nice."

Faye walked over to Amber. Linking arms, they walked to the kitchen together.

"I was just reading Jesus' words in the Sermon on the Mount. He was telling everyone listening not to worry about what you will eat or what clothes you will wear. God knows we need them and if we seek Him first, He will provide everything we need."

"What if you're worrying about people looking for you?"

"Well, Jesus simply said, 'Do not worry about tomorrow, for tomorrow will worry about itself. Each day has enough trouble of its own.'"

"So at midnight I can worry about tomorrow?"

Faye laughed as she grabbed a pot and poured milk into it. "Not quite. Jesus asked the question, 'Can any one of you by worrying add a single hour to your life?' And then He said something interesting to me. He said, 'Since you cannot do this very little thing, why do you worry about the rest?'"

"Adding hours to our lives is simple to God?"

"It is, as simple as me making this hot chocolate. And since He can so easily do something that seems so impossible to us, then taking care of whatever problems may come tomorrow will be that much easier for Him."

"It's a trust issue," said Amber. "I heard you say you would make hot chocolate and I know from experience that you do what you say. So I don't worry about whether or not I will get any."

"Or if you'll want it when it's done."

Amber thought for a few moments. "But my experience with God is so limited."

"That's precisely what God and I were talkin' about when you came down."

"And did He give you any answers?"

"One thing you need to learn is that God loves to give wisdom. The book of James says that God gives it generously to those who ask for it. Another thing you should know is that He put us here to live and work together. You may not have much experience with God yet, but He's surrounded you with people who do."

"Like when you lost Jamie?"

"Yes, that, and lots of other things. And don't forget all He's brought Peter and Andy through too. My son loves God and has put Him to the test more than once. He knows God's provision pretty well. And Andy would never purposely let Peter down."

Faye brought two steamy mugs of hot chocolate over to the breakfast bar and sat down beside Amber. "I promise you that those two boys are praying tonight and they will protect you with everything they've got as events unfold tomorrow."

Amber looked down at her mug. "I love him."

"I know that." Faye covered Amber's hand with her own.

"I don't want to mess up his life. I know I can be a liability."

"Now I don't know of a single person here who thinks of any part of you as a liability. Goodness, Frank's already given you a nickname, which is his way of saying you belong. Brittney's been talking all week about coming down for New Year's Eve so she can spend more time with you. Allie can't wait to work with you, and Andy certainly wouldn't have gone to Peter first about this Matthew if he wasn't trying to protect you."

"But do you think I'm right for Peter?" Amber looked at Faye. "I want to know what you really think."

"Amber, I could give you all kinds of signs, changes in Peter since you came. He's a better man today than he was two months ago. You gave him something to fight for, something to live for. You brought a new purpose into his heart. Dear one, I not only think you are the right one for my boy, but I thank God that He brought you into our lives."

Amber, touched by Faye's words, wrapped her arms around Faye's neck. She couldn't remember the last hug she had willingly offered, but this felt right. *Thank You, God.*

✕◇✕◇✕◇✕◇✕◇✕◇✕◇✕◇

As Amber descended the stairs in the morning, she saw Peter in the kitchen quietly talking to his mom. She stood watching him for a moment, her heart warming at the sight of him. *I can't believe he wants me!*

Sassy ran ahead of her to greet Peter.

"Hey, Sass," he said as he rubbed her ears. He looked up at Amber. "Good morning."

"Morning," said Amber.

"My goodness," said Faye. "I didn't expect you this early."

"I couldn't sleep any longer."

"Still worried?" said Faye.

"A little," said Amber.

"Andy will call as soon as he knows anything," said Peter. "He was going to call Matthew about nine."

"Can you be here when he calls?" said Amber.

"I've already cleared my day," said Peter.

"Well, come on, then," said Faye. "Let's get some breakfast in you."

"And some more coffee in me," said Peter.

Amber appreciated the effort Faye and Peter were making to keep her mind occupied on other things, but her eyes kept wandering back to the clock. When the phone rang at a quarter after nine, she jumped. Peter looked at her then went to the phone.

"Hello? Yeah. . . . Okay . . ."

Amber's heart pounded. She desperately wanted to know what was being said on the other end of the phone, but she also wanted to go back to yesterday, before she knew anyone was looking for her. She sank down on the floor beside Sassy and rubbed her ears. "Want to trade places, girl?"

"All right. We'll see you then." Peter hung up the phone and went to sit on the ottoman near Amber. Faye sat down in the chair across from them.

"We're going to meet at Andy's office today at 1:00."

"So soon?" said Faye.

Amber nibbled on her bottom lip.

"They're just in Portland. They pushed for sooner," said Peter as he looked toward Amber, "but Andy refused. He wanted you to have a little time to process this."

"Who's looking for me? Who are we meeting?"

Peter gently took Amber's hand. "Your parents."

"Both of them?" Amber wasn't sure what to do with this knowledge. If her dad was still drinking, she didn't want to go see him. *But Mom was so weak when I left that she couldn't have gotten Dad to go along with the search. Why do they care to find me?*

"Amber?" said Peter.

"I just . . . I don't know." She held tight onto the security his hand offered. "I have good memories of my dad, but they are all from when I was little. From the time Cassie died, Dad was a mean drunk and Mom was a weakling. Why would they be looking for me?"

"Maybe they've changed," said Faye.

Amber got up and stood looking in the direction of Mt. Hood. Some of her dad's words still echoed in her mind. "I'm not sure I can believe that."

"Truth has little to do with belief," said Faye. "The sky is blue whether I believe it or not. Just try to go into this meeting with an open mind and see what God has waiting for you. He just might surprise you."

"How about a walk?" said Peter.

Amber turned and looked at him. "That would be nice."

Chapter 19

P ETER LET AMBER LEAD THE way, and she picked the familiar path to his mom's favorite spot.

"Talk about something," said Amber.

"What do you want to hear about?"

"Tell me about college. Where did you go?"

"I went to Oregon State University over in Corvallis."

"How far away is that?"

"Just a couple hours southwest of here. I was home most weekends."

"And you studied trees?"

Peter laughed. "I guess you could sum it up that way. My degree is in Forest Operations Management. It's kind of a blend of Forest Engineering and Business Management, so I not only had to learn to identify the trees and get a decent understanding of how the forest works but also take courses like Accounting and Business Law."

"You were training yourself to take over your dad's business."

"Yeah. I've always loved it out here. Learning more about the forest fulfilled my curiosity and learning about business just made sense. Andy steps in with the more detailed law stuff, and Allie's degree in accounting has kept Dad out of trouble with the IRS and Department of Revenue. God's always provided the people we needed."

"Have you always known you wanted to do this?"

"Pretty much. I thought about the military for a short time. Many of Mom and Dad's brothers were in active duty because of the draft. One uncle died in Vietnam. But I just couldn't see myself leaving my family behind."

Amber nodded. "I can't see myself leaving your family either."

Peter looked at her. "What do you mean?"

Amber stopped at the edge of the river and watched the water flow. "I know that life is going to have its bumps and rough spots. But your family has showed me for the first time ever that problems can bring a family closer together. I know if my parents had walked back into my life six weeks ago, I would have left town before a meeting could be set up." She turned to look at Peter. "But today, I walk forward to meet them because people like your mom and dad are praying and because you give me courage."

Peter shook his head. "God gives courage. I just remind you of His promises."

Amber looked back at the river. "Millions of drops of water, united in purpose to get to their destination. That's your family, Peter. Your mom and dad, Brittney, Pops, Logan, and Heather. Even friends like Andy and Allie join in the effort. I like being part of that."

She turned back to Peter, looking into his eyes. "And I like that marriage to you is an option in our future."

Peter felt lighter than air. His heart soared as he struggled to control his emotions. He wanted to burst with excitement and run shouting through the forest. *She can be mine. Father, I'm sorry I doubted You again. Thank You! Thank You!*

With a huge smile on his face, He grabbed Amber's hand with both of his own and held it to his chest. He stood for a moment, just taking in her eyes and face.

Then, without letting go of her hand, he turned and said, "How about we walk a little more then get some lunch with Mom before driving into town to meet Andy. He wanted us there early so we could all pray before your parents arrived."

"That sounds good."

Peter turned and led her alongside the river. "You know, OSU offers online classes."

"Are you thinking about taking some?"

"No. I was just thinking that if you liked doing the bookwork in the office, maybe we should check out the online accounting classes."

"I didn't even finish high school, Peter. You really think I'm cut out for college classes?"

"Why not do some training with Allie and think about it? If you want to try a class or two, I'll help where I can, and once you get in over my head, we'll call in Allie. She loves the chance to laugh at my accounting skills, and who knows? Maybe I'll learn more helping you through it than I learned going through it myself!"

Amber laughed at this. "No promises. Let me get through my parents first then we'll see if whatever Allie throws at me makes any sense."

"Deal."

<><><><><><><><><><><><><>

Peter focused on the road ahead as he continued to pray over the afternoon. Amber sat in the seat beside him, quietly looking out the side window. He imagined his mom was also praying as she sat in the seat behind Amber.

He made his way around the square and parked beside Andy's Jeep. *Good. No unfamiliar vehicles.* He looked at Amber. "Ready?"

She nodded and moved to get out of the Jeep. Peter got out and met the ladies on the sidewalk.

"Your dad is supposed to meet me at Micah's," said Faye. "We'll just wait for you there." Faye gave Amber one final hug, squeezed Peter's hand, and turned to walk toward the hardware store.

A teenager zipped around Peter on his skateboard. "Billy!"

The boy came to an abrupt stop. "Yes, sir?"

"Will you walk my mom over to Micah's?"

"Yes, sir. Be happy to." Billy stomped his skateboard and popped it up so he could carry it then ran over to Faye and fell into step beside her.

Peter grabbed Amber's hand and said, "Let's go."

Allie greeted them inside, giving Amber a quick hug before ushering them into Andy's office. Andy sat at his desk talking on the phone.

"Yes, Mrs. Guire," said Andy.

"Go ahead and have a seat," said Allie. "He's been trying to get off the phone with her for ten minutes."

"Mrs. Guire, I understand that, but if you will stop speeding down Main Street, Sheriff Daniel will stop giving you tickets."

Peter directed Amber to the chairs in front of Andy's u-shaped wood desk while Allie sat on the couch beside it. Her trim khaki dress pants, white blouse, and black cardigan gave her a very professional appearance. Only the blonde curly hair she left down hinted at the spunk she harnessed underneath the business attire.

"No, ma'am," Andy continued. "I don't have my calendar in front of me. I'll put you on hold and Rose will pick up and tell you when a good time to come would be. Right now I need to go, as I have another client waiting for me. . . . Yes, ma'am."

Andy pushed a button and asked Rose to take care of Mrs. Guire then looked at Peter and Amber. "Sorry about that. She can be—"

"Andy, be nice," said Allie, smiling at her husband.

"Yes, ma'am," said Andy.

Peter smiled, thinking about the last time he'd tried to help Mrs. Guire pick out a Christmas tree. He was certain he'd held up every tree on the lot for her inspection at least twice.

"Are you ready, Amber?" said Andy.

She sighed. "As ready as I'm going to be, I guess."

"We'll all stay in here until they arrive," said Andy. "Rose will show them into the conference room and then buzz me. We'll all walk in together, Allie and I first, then you and Peter. If at any point you need a break, just nod at me and you and Peter can exit. I'll follow you out to see what you think, then I'll go back in and say whatever needs said. Okay?"

"Okay," said Amber.

"The conference room isn't large," Andy continued, "but at least you'll have a table between you and them. Rose will sit them facing the door, so you'll also have direct access to the exit."

Amber just nodded.

"Al, I want you to go in first and take the chair at the far end of the table. Amber, you take the chair in the middle and Peter and I will sit on either side of you. Any questions?"

Peter looked at Amber as she shook her head.

"All right, then. Why don't we say one more prayer before we go in?"

Andy's phone buzzed and Peter heard Rose's voice. "The Griffins are here."

"Thank you, Rose," said Andy. "Go ahead and show them into the conference room. I'll be there in just a couple minutes."

The intercom clicked off. "Pete, want to pray?"

Peter grabbed Amber's hand and felt it trembling. He bowed his head. "Father, we may wonder what You are doing, but we know that You are in control. Thank You for going ahead of us into this meeting. Daddy, we ask that You provide whatever is needed, including courage and grace. I ask that You give Amber peace as she steps out in faith and trusts You. Allow her to see Your purpose in this. Give Andy great wisdom as he seeks to both protect Amber and mediate the discussion. And, Father, let the outcome be blessed with Your results. In Jesus' name we pray. Amen."

Andy and Allie both echoed Peter's "Amen" and then Andy looked at Amber. "Okay?"

Peter felt her tighten her grip on his hand.

"Let's do this," she said.

Chapter 20

FRANK PACED AT THE STOREFRONT windows.

"Frank, you're going to owe Micah wood for his floor if you don't stop," said Faye. "Come sit down."

"I got wood," said Frank.

"Let him be, Faye. The floor'll be fine."

"What time is it?" said Frank.

"Probably about two minutes past the last time you asked," said Faye.

"It's 12:58, Frank."

"Franklin Yager," said Faye. "Where's your trust in God with this?"

"Trust I got. It's patience I'm lackin'."

The front door opened and two people entered. "Care if we join the party?"

"Brittney!" said Faye.

"After you called, Mom, I called Pops. He refused to wait at home. He said if I didn't bring him down, he was hitchin' a ride with the first delivery man he could find."

"Pops! What on earth?" said Frank.

"That girl's got spunk. I see no sense waitin' at home. Peter's gone with her?"

"Yes, Pops," said Faye. "Peter, Andy, and Allie are all with her."

"Well, then. Where's the coffee, Micah?" said Pops.

Brittney just rolled her eyes as Micah led Pops to the back of the store to grab a mug. "Whatever happens, Mom, one of us must call Heather right away. She's pacing the floor at home with a teething baby, although I don't know if the pacing is more for Heather or the baby. She's been calling me about every ten minutes."

Chapter 21

ANDY OPENED THE CONFERENCE ROOM door and Allie walked in before him. Amber paused a moment and then walked through the door, heading straight for her chair.

"Rachel!" said her mom, Victoria.

Amber stopped behind the chair and looked across the table at a woman she barely recognized. *She looks old.*

Peter reached around to pull out her chair. She half-consciously sat as Peter took his place beside her. Her mother's short brown hair and pale skin looked familiar, but something was different. *She almost glows. Is it just because she's found me? Or is it for real? Is she truly happy?*

"Rachel," said her father, Thomas. "It is so good to see you."

Amber looked at her father, who also seemed to have aged considerably. At just forty-eight years old, he nevertheless had completely gray hair, and his tanned face boasted many wrinkles. *Wrinkles in all the right places from smiling. Could they both be happy? Could things have changed that much?*

"Why don't we start with introductions?" said Andy. "Mr. and Mrs. Griffin, you clearly recognize Miss Griffin. This is a friend, Peter Yager, and my assistant and wife, Mrs. Williams.

Perhaps it would be best if you began by telling us what you hope to accomplish."

"Mr. Williams, we want nothing more than to reestablish contact with our daughter," said Thomas.

"And your private detective?" said Andy.

"Matthew just helped us search," said Victoria. "Rachel, you were so hard to find. When you left, you just disappeared. The police barely found any trace of you."

"You called the police?" said Amber. That surprised her.

"Rachel," said Thomas, "I know I was a horrible father those last few years. I didn't know what to do after . . . I-I-I was so lost after . . ."

"You can say it," said Amber. "After Cassie died. Your world was Cassie, and when she died your world fell apart."

"That's not entirely true!" said Thomas.

"Rachel, we loved you," said Victoria.

"Maybe, but you loved your grief more." Amber could feel the tears coming but she didn't care. *These people are not going to waltz into my life and play the long lost parents!*

Everyone was quiet for a moment. Allie grabbed a box of tissues from the windowsill behind her and offered them to Amber and then Victoria.

"We deserve that," said Thomas.

"Are you living nearby?" said Andy.

Thomas looked at Andy. "We have an apartment in Portland." He shifted his focus back to Amber. "We've stayed pretty mobile the last eight years, moving occasionally as we could find traces of you."

"You've been following me for eight years?"

"We first moved to Fresno about seven years ago," said Thomas, "then Sacramento about five years ago. Two years ago we moved to Eugene, and the end of May to Portland."

"Whenever we found a lead that sounded credible, we followed it," said Victoria.

"What about Ryan and Keith?" said Amber. "You dragged them around too?" She couldn't believe how closely they'd followed her path. *They've been a lot closer to me than I ever thought.*

"After you left," said Thomas, "I realized how much I'd let the family down. I'd lost both my girls, your mom was always sick, and Ryan was starting to get into trouble. I knew I had to make a major change or risk losing everyone. One night, I was walking around the park trying my best not to go to the liquor store. I met a man. He talked to me, really listened to me." Thomas looked at Victoria, grabbing the hand she offered him. "Turns out he was a deacon at your grandparents' church."

Amber jumped out of her seat and turned to the door. *This is too much. Now they get to play the church card too!*

"Rachel!" said Victoria. "Wait!"

Before she reached the door, Peter was at her side. He held her firmly by the shoulders. "Hear him out." His voice was quiet, calming. His eyes were steady.

Everything in her wanted to walk away. She closed her eyes. *He's caused me so much pain, God.*

Yes. But some that you blame him for, you caused yourself.

She sighed deeply. Breathing for a moment to calm her emotions, she looked at Peter. "Okay."

She turned and caught Andy's eye. He had turned in his chair, ready to follow her. She nodded at him but remained standing with her back to Peter.

"Sorry," said Amber to Thomas. "Please continue."

He was standing, eyes pleading with her. "Rachel, I know I lost your trust. When I asked Jesus to take control of my life, it was pretty messed up. But He came in and over time helped me fix my marriage and become a better father to the boys. I know it's asking a lot of you to give me a chance to rebuild our relationship. But that's all I want."

"Do you drink?" said Amber.

"No alcohol," said Thomas.

"Ever?" said Amber.

"I've been clean for nine years, eight months."

Amber sighed again. *Now what, God?*

Try.

I don't know if I want to.

Look at Peter. Love is worth the risk. Try.

Amber closed her eyes for a moment and leaned into Peter's strength. Giving them a chance seemed like a big risk, but Frank had risked a lot on her too. *Okay, God.*

"There's a New Year's Eve party at the house where I live," said Amber. "It's their family and a couple close friends. You can show up about six tomorrow night. Andy, can you give them directions?"

"Of course," said Andy.

Victoria stood, her eyes misty. "Thank you, Rachel."

Amber turned to leave, then looked back. "I go by Amber now."

"Okay, Ra-Amber" said Victoria.

Amber walked out the door and felt Peter grab her trembling hand. Her emotions were a jumble and tears flooded her eyes.

"Rose, we'll be in Andy's office for a bit," said Peter.

She followed his lead as the sobs began. She felt herself being guided onto the couch then cradled in Peter's arms. He held her tight as she cried out her fear, anger, and stress.

◇◇◇◇◇◇◇◇◇◇◇◇◇◇◇◇◇

"Are you ready to face the world again?" said Peter.

Amber sighed as she looked at the pile of tissues beside her. "I feel like I owe Andy a couple boxes of tissues."

Peter laughed and pulled her up off the couch. Her eyes rested on the large wet spot on his shoulder. "And you a new shirt! Oh, Peter, I'm sorry."

"Don't be. I cherished the moments holding you, and with my coat on, no one will know it's there but me."

How did he know I was nervous about anyone seeing that? she wondered.

He helped her into her coat then slipped on his own before opening the door.

"Finally!" said Pops.

"Pops!" said Brittney.

Amber looked into the faces of Frank, Faye, Pops, Brittney, Micah, Andy, and Allie all sitting or standing around Andy's front office. "What are you all doing here?"

"Couldn't wait," said Pops.

"We saw them leave," said Faye, "and we didn't see you come out. We got worried."

"Impatient," said Frank.

"And Andy lawyered up on us," said Brittney. "Wouldn't tell us a thing."

Andy just raised his hands in defense.

"So what happened, dear-heart?" said Frank.

Brittney's phone rang. "Hang on. Oh, it's Heather. Wait! I'll put her on speaker."

Amber just laughed as she looked up at Peter.

"You might want to remember," he whispered in her ear, "that I come as a package deal."

She just shook her head. "And what a package it is."

"What's that mean?" said Pops.

Amber smiled broadly. "It means that I have never felt so loved. Okay, the quick version is that shortly after I left, Dad found Jesus, got clean, and fixed the family he still had. Now they want a chance to be part of my life."

"What did you say?" said Faye.

"I invited them to your house tomorrow night. Is that all right?"

"Absolutely!"

"Goodness!" said Amber. "I didn't think to ask about my brothers. I don't know if it will just be them, or if Ryan and Keith will be there too."

"What, like Mom won't have enough food for them and sixteen others beside?" said Brittney.

"Not if I don't get home and get to cookin'," said Faye. "Come on, now. We need to let Andy get back to work. Mrs. Guire's called three times while we've been sitting here!"

As everyone began filing out onto the sidewalk, Amber walked over to Andy and Allie. "Thank you."

Allie gave her a hug. "You did great. I'm proud to call you my friend."

Amber smiled. "Thanks."

Peter reached out and shook Andy's hand. "Thanks, man."

"Anytime, Pete. See you tomorrow."

Chapter 22

"HEY, MOM!" PETER CAME IN the door loaded down with bags.

"Peter! What on earth have you got?" said Faye.

He grinned. "Fireworks!"

Faye laughed at him. "In some ways you boys just never grow up. Your dad was hoping you'd think to get some!"

"I got some sparklers for the kids plus some cone fountains we can light in the yard."

"Go put them on top of the washer or something for later tonight."

"Okay. Where's Amber and Sass?"

"Curled up in there with Brittney, Heather, and the kids. Taylor needed a nap but wouldn't slow down long enough to fall asleep. So all the girls piled up with pillows and blankets and popped in a movie. Last time I walked through, Emma and Heather were down but Taylor was still goin' strong."

"I'll go check on them."

Peter walked into the living room. The movie was coming to an end, the prince claiming his princess, and everyone was asleep except for Amber and two-year-old Taylor. They were curled up, totally entranced by the movie.

"Did you see that Am-er? Did you see that?"

"I did."

"I wuv dat moo-vee." She patted Amber's cheek. "Do you wuv dat moo-vee?"

"I do, Taylor. How about we go see what Grandma's doing and let Mommy and Aunt Brittney sleep, okay?"

Taylor dutifully nodded her head and turned to get up. Peter crouched down, putting his finger to his lips to remind her to be quiet when she saw him. Her eyes lit up and she scrambled into his arms.

"Unc Pe-er!"

"How's my blonde beauty?"

"Her watch Belle wif me."

"I know. I saw you."

He looked over at Amber's sparkling eyes and held out his hand to her. She put her hand in his and they walked together back to the kitchen.

"Taylor Faith," said Faye. "You are supposed to be sleeping."

"Mommy sleep."

Faye laughed. "Yes, Mommy needs the sleep after being up so much last night with your baby sister."

"I know, Taylor," said Peter. "How about we get your coat and mittens and we go build a snowman."

"Yeah!" Taylor threw her little arms up in the air. "I need my mit-ens, Am-er. And my hat!"

Amber giggled at the child. "Come on." Amber reached for Taylor, who gladly went to her. "You and I will go get our coats on, and we'll let Uncle Peter find something to be the snow-man's eyes and nose."

"And my mit-ens too."

Peter watched Amber carry the child out to the mudroom to get ready for outside, Taylor chattering away. Part of him wanted to be selfish and keep Amber to himself, but watching her with Taylor. . . . *First things first, Pete. Have a fun afternoon, help tonight with her parents go smoothly, and then the two gifts.*

"What are you thinking, son?" said Frank, walking into the kitchen.

"Huh? Oh, nothing, Dad."

"Yeah, nothing," said Faye. "He's thinking about a beautiful brunette carrying a cute little blonde. That's all."

"Hmmm," said Frank. "Uh huh."

"What?" Peter tried to feign innocence but knew he failed miserably. Covering up his smile, he said, "You got any long carrots, Mom? What about something that can be eyes?"

<hr />

After building a snowman, Taylor finally started giving into sleep in the middle of her snow angel. Peter carried her inside and held her while Amber took off her snow boots, coat, and mittens.

"Am-er hold me?"

"Just a minute sweetheart." Amber kicked off her boots and tossed her coat onto a hook then gently took Taylor from Peter. They were just walking into the kitchen as Heather came in from the living room.

"She's just falling asleep," said Peter.

"Thank you for letting me nap," said Heather. She took the sleeping child and headed off to lay her down.

"You two want some hot chocolate?" said Faye.

"That sounds wonderful," said Amber.

"You got any coffee?" said Peter.

"I just started a new pot. Should be ready in two or three minutes. Here you go, Amber."

"Thank you. So what happens at a New Year's celebration around here?"

"Well, with Pops, we have to make sure we follow some of the Danish traditions," said Faye. "We've modified them some but one he insists on is having boiled cod for dinner. The marzipan ring cake you helped me make last night is also a requirement. Peter brought some fireworks for when it gets dark, and this year, we get to throw dishes!"

Peter groaned.

"Throw dishes?" said Amber.

"Mom."

"Peter Flemming. You're whining."

"Throw dishes?" said Amber.

"You've known since you started that house what Pops wanted to do once you moved in," said Faye.

"Ugh," said Peter.

Amber pulled on Peter's sleeve. "Throw dishes?"

"It's another one of Pops's Danish traditions," said Peter.

"In Denmark," said Faye, "friends come by and throw old dishes at your doorstep to wish you many friends and good relationships. As Pops's family began to Americanize here, they changed the tradition so that it is only done when a family member moves into a new home."

"I'll be picking up broken glass for weeks," said Peter.

"Yes, you will," said Faye.

Amber giggled.

"Are we laughing at Peter's expense?" said Brittney.

"I thought you were sleeping," said Peter.

"Oh, that means we are," said Brittney, walking over to wrap her arm around Faye. "Tell me all!"

"We're breaking dishes tonight at Peter's house," said Amber.

"Oh! That's right," said Brittney. "Yeah! Someone else's turn to clean up broken pottery!"

"Not funny, Britt," said Peter, as everyone in the kitchen laughed.

~~~~~~~~~~~~~~~~~~~

Peter looked at the clock. *5:45. Where's Amber?*

"I need to get up, munchkin." He kissed the top of Emma's head and handed her off to Logan. He walked into the kitchen. "Mom, where's Amber?"

"I think she just walked outside."

Peter grabbed his shoes and walked onto the back deck. Amber was standing at the railing. "You okay?"

She smiled at him. "Yeah. Just getting a little antsy. How will I know they are being genuine and not just play acting for me?"

"Trust the Holy Spirit to guide you. And you don't have to figure this out all by yourself. Everyone here is willing to pray with you and seek the truth. And if you haven't noticed, they don't tend to be quiet about their feelings."

Amber smiled. "That's true."

"Plus," said Peter, "can you imagine being your parents, walking into that house full of people?"

"It's as bad as Thanksgiving in there!"

"Almost." Peter smiled at her. "A large part of me believes they are genuine. I think God just might be working to bring your family back together."

Amber sighed. "Maybe." She turned to look at all the activity on the other side of the French doors. "Just tell me something."

"Anything."

"Do parties around here slow down after the New Year?"

Peter laughed. "Not a chance. There's Martin Luther King Day, President's Day, National Pancake Day. . . ."

Amber giggled. "Okay, okay. I get it."

Brittney opened one of the doors. "They're here."

Peter looked at Amber. "Ready?"

"I think so. I think I'm ready to give them an honest chance."

"I knew you could."

Chapter 23

PETER AND AMBER TOSSED THEIR shoes into the mud-room and walked into the living room. Logan was gathering coats from everyone while Faye was taking care of introductions.

"Andy," said Peter. "Thanks for bringing them out."

"Did I miss anything?" said Andy.

"Just the usual chaos," said Peter.

"Ah, here she is," said Faye. Faye put her arm around Amber and brought her forward to see her mom and dad.

Amber looked at a lanky young man standing behind her mom. His brown hair was just slightly darker than hers, and his nose and mouth looked exactly like her dad's. "Keith?"

"Hey," said Keith. "Long time, huh?"

Amber stood uncertainly. Part of her longed to hug her brother, but he was so unfamiliar to her. She hadn't seen him since he was six years old and now this teenager stood before her.

"Yes," she said. "Very long."

"Well, everyone come in and make yourselves at home," said Faye. "Dinner will be ready in about ten minutes."

"What do you need help with, Mom?" said Brittney.

"I'll come, too," said Allie.

"Why don't you come and sit in here," said Peter to Thomas and Victoria. "I don't know if Andy told you, but this is my parents' house."

"He told us we'd be coming to spend the evening with your family," said Thomas as he sat on the couch. "Thank you for allowing us to intrude."

"It's no intrusion," said Frank, sitting in the chair to his left. "My wife loves a party. The more people she can get crowded in here, the happier she is."

Amber crossed in front of the couch and sat on the ottoman in front of the fire, allowing Peter to have the chair behind her. Sassy came and lay at her feet, keeping a watchful eye on the new people, while Andy, Logan, and Heather quietly made their way to the kitchen.

"Amber," said Victoria, "you look wonderful."

"Thanks. Living here has been good for me in a lot of ways."

"I'm thankful for that," said Victoria.

"She's helped my wife lots, both here at the house and the office," said Frank.

"Did I understand Mr. Williams to say you own a logging business?"

"Started it 'bout thirty years ago now," said Frank. "Hard to believe it's been that long."

"Yes," said Thomas, looking back at Amber. "Time certainly does go by quickly."

"Is that your dog, sis?" said Keith.

Amber's "no" and Peter's "yes" had Thomas and Victoria looking at each other and Frank chuckling.

Amber looked at Peter and giggled. She reached down to rub Sassy's head. "Well, sort of, I guess. She was Peter's dog when I first got here. I was afraid of her because of another dog a couple years ago. But she insisted on hanging close to me."

"She traded allegiances," said Peter.

"Uncle Peter!" Emma raced into the room and launched herself onto the arm of his chair. "Grandma says come to dinner!"

"Am-er. You sit by me?" Taylor came running in behind Emma, squeezing past her to get to Amber. She patted Amber's cheeks. "You sit by me, 'kay?"

Amber smiled. "Okay, Taylor."

"Well, folks," said Frank as he led the way to the dining room. "It will be a bit tight with all of us in there, but we tried it at Thanksgivin' and everyone survived."

Dinner was a lively affair and afterward all the ladies pitched in to help clean up. Peter, Logan, and Andy went out to set up the fireworks while Frank, Pops, Thomas, and Keith got a blaze going in the fire pit on the porch.

"We're all set up outside, Mom, as soon as you're ready," said Peter.

"Okay," said Faye. "Amber, why don't you grab the marshmallows for the kids—"

"Grandma! You got marshmallows?" said Emma. She went running to the living room. "Taylor! Grandma got marshmallows!"

Everyone giggled as little Taylor cried, "Yeah!"

"Come on, girls," said Heather. "Let's get your boots and coats on."

"Give me Megan," said Brittney.

Amber stood beside her mom. "How old are the girls?" said Victoria.

"Emma is four, Taylor two, and Megan is almost eight months," said Amber.

"They seem very attached to the whole family, including you."

"Faye likes parties and she loves family. Logan and Heather live on this side of Portland, so it's only about forty-five minutes to their house. They get to come down a lot."

"And Brittney is a sister?"

"Yep. She lives in Portland, too, close to Pops, which is Frank's dad."

"And Peter lives down here?"

Amber began to lead the way out the French doors. "Yes. He has a house just a short walk away."

"He seems nice."

"The whole family is. Honestly, I don't think I'd be standing here talking to you if it weren't for them."

"Then I owe them a great deal."

"Can I interest you ladies in a sparkler?" said Andy.

"Sure," said Victoria. "Thank you."

Amber took one and both ladies held them out as Andy lit the ends. Suddenly Peter was in front of her holding Taylor.

"Come wats fir-works, Am-er."

Amber smiled at her. "I don't have my coat, Taylor. I'll get cold away from the fire."

"No, you won't. I keep you warm," said Taylor.

Peter grinned down at her. "You take Taylor and I'll get your coat. Would you like yours, Mrs. Griffin?"

"Yes, thank you, Peter."

Amber grabbed Taylor and walked to the railing so they could see the fireworks. Peter came back with coats and held Taylor so Amber could put hers on.

With the family lined up at the railing, Logan and Keith started lighting the fountains. It was very surreal to Amber. Emma squealed in delight while Taylor peeked out from Peter's neck. A scene so familiar, yet so different. She looked at her parents, her mom leaning into her dad as they watched the flickering lights. They seemed at peace with the horror of that night so long ago. Strangely, the tightness that always came to her chest at New Year's Eve was missing.

Peter looked at her. "You okay?"

She smiled back at him. "I am."

He turned to Andy beside him. "Taylor, go to Andy for a minute."

The little girl traded arms and Peter turned to look fully at Amber. "I know this night has a lot of bad memories for you, but I'd like this to be the first of many good ones."

"It is. I—" Amber stopped abruptly as she realized Peter was holding out an open ring box to her. A beautiful diamond solitaire sparkled in the moonlight.

"I meant it when I told you that I would not rush you down the aisle," said Peter. "You may pick whatever date you like. But I want the world to know you are mine. Amber, will you marry me?"

Tears overflowed and Peter gently wiped some away. Amber giggled. "I think I've cried more in the last few weeks then I have in years."

"Does that mean yes?" said Pops.

"Hush and let them have their moment," said Faye.

Amber laughed.

"Don't know if I should remind you that the circus behind me is part of the deal," said Peter.

"I love the deal," said Amber. "And I love you. Yes, I will marry you."

Peter took the ring from its case and slipped it on her finger. "In our family, the ring traditionally comes with a second gift."

Frank walked over with a package and handed it to Peter. "Thanks, Dad." He handed it carefully to Amber. "With my heart."

She unwrapped the gift and found a blue leather-bound Bible. On the front cover was stamped "To My Beloved RAY."

"It says 'To My Beloved,'" said Peter, "because it's from both God and me to you, and you are most certainly our beloved. But when we get married, my precious one, your initials will change to R-A-Y. You are not only my beloved, you are my ray from Heaven."

"Oh, Peter," said Amber. "I just don't know what to say." She held the Bible to her chest. *I don't remember receiving a more precious gift.*

Taylor tapped Peter on the shoulder. "Unc Pe-er?"

He turned to look at her, "Yes, Taylor?"

"Does it mean Am-er family now?"

Peter smiled at Amber and reached for her hand. "Yes, Taylor. Amber's family now."

"Yeah!" said Taylor, her little arms stretched high.

As everyone giggled, Pops spoke up. "Good. Now we can do a proper dish throwing!"

Peter groaned as Amber laughed. "Come on, grumpy. I've never been part of a dish throwing before."

Chapter 24

PETER GROANED MORE WHEN BRITTNEY pulled up in front of his house in her Chevy Equinox and revealed several boxes of dishes in the trunk. "What did you do?"

"Wasn't me!" said Brittney. "But as I helped Pops load them up he mentioned cleaning out a couple of thrift stores."

"Pops!"

"What? Didn't know you's gonna ask this fine young lady to marry you tonight," said Pops as he put his arm around Amber. "Figured you needed all the well-wishin' you could get!"

Peter tried his best to not think about the dings he was certain he'd find on and around his front door as everyone joined in the festivities. Even Amber's parents tossed a dish or two at the threshold.

As the last dish was finally tossed, Frank came up to his son, placing a hand on his shoulder. "Don't think about the marks in the wood, son. They're just markers on the journey."

"And we didn't break any windows!" said Logan.

Peter laughed. "I appreciate that!"

"So when do we get to see inside?" said Faye.

"How about now, Mom?"

Peter led the way up the front steps, unlocking the door and flipping on lights. He welcomed everyone in but focused on Amber as she wandered around, taking in the details of what would one day be her home too. He joined her, Faye, and Victoria at the kitchen opening.

"Well?" he said.

"Peter. It's beautiful," said Faye.

"You did all this?" said Amber.

"Most of it," said Peter. "Logan and Andy helped a lot and I had professionals come in to install a couple of things."

"You're very good, Peter," said Victoria. "This is a beautiful home."

Peter held out his hand to Amber. "I want to show you something."

He led her up the circular staircase placed strategically to separate the living and dining areas and into a loft over the dining room and kitchen. An open railing allowed her to see the living room below and out the large windows situated on the upper half of the front wall. Two skylights, one on each side of the roof, would allow in more sunlight during the day.

"I thought you could use this as a studio," said Peter.

She looked at him. "A studio?"

"Yeah, for your drawing. Or as an office if you decide to head back to school."

"You designed all this for me?"

Peter walked the two steps to her side and took both her hands in his. "I originally started this house for my family. But late last summer I was frustrated. I watched Logan and Heather with the girls and felt like my dream would never come. Then you walked into our lives. Shortly after you arrived, I began to hope. And as I learned more about you, I modified the plans."

"What do you mean?"

"You helped in little things. Like when I saw every shirt you looked at while Christmas shopping was blue, I purchased blue paint for the walls."

"And the large walk-in closet in the master bedroom?"

"I know how Mom shops for Britt."

She took a step closer to him. "And the two bedrooms on the other side?"

"That goes back to my dreams for a family. Sound okay to you?"

"Oh, yes. Peter, I don't know that I could have imagined a better home. I love it."

They walked back downstairs and joined the rest of the family. Emma lay sleeping on the couch, and Taylor was quickly fading in Logan's arms.

"Nice job, Peter," said Allie.

"Very impressive," said Thomas.

"Still needs a woman's touch," said Frank.

"Here, here," said Pops.

"You two shush," said Faye. "He's working on that just fine."

Amber walked over to the front window and looked out at the starlit night. "Can we add one thing?"

"What are you missing, my Ray?" said Peter.

She turned and smiled at him, then looked at Faye. "I'd like to plant a maple tree out front."

◇×◇×◇×◇×◇×◇×◇×◇×◇×◇×◇

The hour was late as everyone walked back from Peter's house. Logan gathered the girls' toys and began loading them into their vehicle while Heather got the sleepy trio ready to travel. Brittney only stopped long enough to grab Pops's coffee mug before she headed toward Portland.

"Can you folks find the road north okay?" said Andy.

"Yes, I think so," said Thomas. "Thank you for meeting us in town and bringing us out here."

"You're welcome."

"I'm glad you came, . . . Mom," said Amber. She stepped forward and gave her mom a hug. Victoria seemed uncertain what to do at first then wrapped her daughter in her arms. As Amber stepped back, Victoria raised one hand to gently touch her cheek.

"You too, Dad."

Peter watched as Victoria's eyes misted watching her husband hold their daughter. *They've got a real chance, Father. Thank You.*

"If you don't think he'd mind," said Amber, "I'd appreciate the chance to thank Matthew for all the work he did."

"I think he'd like that, don't you, Thomas?" said Victoria.

"I'm sure he would," said Thomas.

"I still have his card here," said Andy. He pulled out his wallet and shuffled through until he found the right one. "Here . . . well, that's strange."

"What?" said Peter.

"Last week this card . . ." Andy stopped.

"Andy?" said Peter. "Last week, what?"

Andy looked at Peter. "His card is how I tracked down the agency. And it's how I called him Tuesday morning."

"What's the problem, Andy?" said Faye.

He turned the card around so everyone could see. The golden words on the card sat in stark contrast to the brilliant white background. No agency name or phone number appeared on the card. It simply said, *Matthew, Hebrews 13:1–2.*

"I knew it!" said Faye as she looked at Frank.

"Knew what, Mom?" said Peter.

"Grab a Bible and look up his reference, son," said Frank.

Amber picked up her new Bible and handed it to Peter. He flipped back to Hebrews and began to read. "Keep on loving one another as brothers and sisters. Do not forget to show hospitality to strangers, for by so doing some people have shown hospitality to angels without knowing it."

◇×◇×◇×◇×◇×◇×◇×◇×◇

Peter sat on the couch with Amber curled up beside him, both watching the fire. Frank sat in one chair gently snoring while Faye sat in the other looking out the windows.

"What a great end to the year," said Faye.

"I agree," said Peter.

"I can't believe how my life has changed," said Amber.

"You still have a lot to tell me, Ray," said Peter.

She looked at him as he continued.

"Like how do I find this dog that terrorized you?"

She laughed.

What a beautiful sound, he thought.

"Oh, Peter," said Faye as she giggled.

"I do have a question," said Amber.

"What's that?" said Peter.

"Not for you, Pete," sad Amber. She looked at Faye. "I'm not sure what to call you. Calling you by your first name just doesn't seem right. You've been such a . . . well, you've been like a mother to me. I'm wondering if I could just call you . . . Momma."

Peter watched as Amber left his mother speechless. She looked at Amber with tears in her eyes.

"Oh, my dear one," said Faye. "I would be honored." She reached out her hand to Amber, who grabbed it and held tight for a moment.

"Well, with that question answered," Amber said as she looked at Peter, "I guess the only question left is how fast can this family put together a wedding?"

Chapter 25

RYAN PULLED UP TO THE firehouse and got out. He walked to his bunk for the next twenty-four hours and threw his stuff into the locker.

"Griffin!"

"Yeah," said Ryan.

"You got a letter."

The fire chief walked up and handed him the envelope.

"Thanks." Ryan looked at the front and recognized his mother's writing. He tore it open to read her newest message.

"Good news?" Ryan's partner for the shift tossed his bag on the bed next to Ryan.

"My sister's getting married in three weeks."

Coming Soon! Ryan's Crossing

WHEN RYAN TRAVELS TO AMBER'S wedding, the life he thought was under control begins to unravel. Can he forgive Amber for leaving him? What does he do with the dark haired beauty that's soon to be his sister-in-law? Could God really have a better plan in mind than the paramedic certification he's worked so hard to earn?

Crossing Values Devotional

LOVE THE STORY? WANT TO go a little deeper? Check out the free 7-Day Devotional at CarrieDaws.com/Freebies. But wait! There's more! This booklet only scratches the surface of the themes hidden within the story. Would you like to write a devotion and have it posted for others to download as well? Just email it to me at Contact@CarrieDaws.com.

Crossing Values Book Club Discussion Sheet

SO YOU WANT TO RECOMMEND to your book club that you read Crossing Values, but then you'd be responsible for coming up with the discussion? Not a problem! Simply download the free Discussion Sheet available at CarrieDaws.com/Freebies and take it along with you.

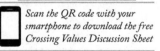

Scan the QR code with your smartphone to download the free Crossing Values Discussion Sheet

For more information about
CARRIE DAWS
&
CROSSING VALUES
please visit:

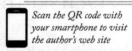

*Scan the QR code with
your smartphone to visit
the author's web site*

www.CarrieDaws.com
Contact@CarrieDaws.com
@CarrieDaws

For more information about
AMBASSADOR INTERNATIONAL
please visit:

www.ambassador-international.com
@AmbassadorIntl
www.facebook.com/AmbassadorIntl